END OF THE HUNT

"You're supposed to be scouting," Laura York said, after she had let Ruff Justice lead her into a stand of oaks. Her fingers toyed with the fringes of his buckskin shirt. He could feel her weight against him, the press of her thigh and pelvis, of her breasts. Her blouse was open at the throat and her cleavage drew his eyes and then his lips.

"Let 'em find their own big cats," Ruff said, and kissed her as his hands drew her to him.

She stepped back and opened her blouse and shrugged out of it to stand there, her pink-budded breasts proud and unashamed to be seen.

Now, wasn't this just about the greatest hunting? Ruff thought, as she came back into touching range....

Wild Westerns by Warren T. Longtree

(0451)
- [ ] RUFF JUSTICE #1: SUDDEN THUNDER (110285—$2.50)
- [ ] RUFF JUSTICE #2: NIGHT OF THE APACHE (110293—$2.50)
- [ ] RUFF JUSTICE #3: BLOOD ON THE MOON (112256—$2.50)
- [ ] RUFF JUSTICE #4: WIDOW CREEK (114221—$2.50)
- [ ] RUFF JUSTICE #5: VALLEY OF GOLDEN TOMBS (115635—$2.50)
- [ ] RUFF JUSTICE #6: THE SPIRIT WOMAN WAR (117832—$2.50)
- [ ] RUFF JUSTICE #7: DARK ANGEL RIDING (118820—$2.50)
- [ ] RUFF JUSTICE #8: THE DEATH OF IRON HORSE (121449—$2.50)
- [ ] RUFF JUSTICE #9: WINDWOLF (122828—$2.50)
- [ ] RUFF JUSTICE #10: SHOSHONE RUN (123883—$2.50)
- [ ] RUFF JUSTICE #11: COMANCHE PEAK (124901—$2.50)
- [ ] RUFF JUSTICE #12: PETTICOAT EXPRESS (127765—$2.50)
- [ ] RUFF JUSTICE #13: POWER LODE (128788—$2.50)
- [ ] RUFF JUSTICE #14: THE STONE WARRIORS (129733—$2.50)
- [ ] RUFF JUSTICE #15: CHEYENNE MOON (131177—$2.50)
- [ ] RUFF JUSTICE #16: HIGH VENGEANCE (132009—$2.50)
- [ ] RUFF JUSTICE #17: DRUM ROLL (132815—$2.50)
- [ ] RUFF JUSTICE #18: THE RIVERBOAT QUEEN (134125—$2.50)
- [ ] RUFF JUSTICE #19: FRENCHMAN'S PASS (135288—$2.50)
- [ ] RUFF JUSTICE #20: THE SONORA BADMAN (136233—$2.75)
- [ ] RUFF JUSTICE #21: THE DENVER DUCHESS (137752—$2.75)

*Price is higher in Canada

Buy them at your local bookstore or use this convenient coupon for ordering.

NEW AMERICAN LIBRARY,
P.O. Box 999, Bergenfield, New Jersey 07621

Please send me the books I have checked above. I am enclosing $_____ (please add $1.00 to this order to cover postage and handling). Send check or money order—no cash or C.O.D.'s. Prices and numbers are subject to change without notice.

Name _____

Address _____

City _____ State _____ Zip Code _____

Allow 4-6 weeks for delivery.
This offer is subject to withdrawal without notice.

RUFF JUSTICE #23

The Death Hunters

by
Warren T. Longtree

A SIGNET BOOK
NEW AMERICAN LIBRARY

PUBLISHER'S NOTE

This novel is a work of fiction. Names, characters, places, and incidents either are the product of the author's imagination or are used fictitiously, and any resemblance to actual persons, living or dead, events, or locales is entirely coincidental.

NAL BOOKS ARE AVAILABLE AT QUANTITY DISCOUNTS WHEN USED TO PROMOTE PRODUCTS OR SERVICES. FOR INFORMATION PLEASE WRITE TO PREMIUM MARKETING DIVISION, NEW AMERICAN LIBRARY, 1633 BROADWAY, NEW YORK, NEW YORK 10019.

Copyright © 1985 by New American Library

All rights reserved

The first chapter of this book appeared in *The Opium Queen*, the twenty-second volume of this series.

SIGNET TRADEMARK REG. U.S. PAT. OFF. AND FOREIGN COUNTRIES
REGISTERED TRADEMARK—MARCA REGISTRADA
HECHO EN CHICAGO, U.S.A.

SIGNET, SIGNET CLASSIC, MENTOR, PLUME, MERIDIAN AND NAL BOOKS are published by New American Library,
1633 Broadway, New York, New York 10019

First Printing, December, 1985

1 2 3 4 5 6 7 8 9

PRINTED IN THE UNITED STATES OF AMERICA

RUFF JUSTICE

He knew the West better than any man alive—a hostile, savage land rife with both violent outlaws and courageous adventurers. But Ruff Justice had a sixth sense that kept him breathing and saw his enemies dead. A scout for the U.S. Cavalry, he was paid to protect the public, and nobody was faster at sniffing out a killer, a crook, a con man—red or white, at close range or far. Anyone on the wrong side of the law would have to reckon with the menace of Ruff's murderously sharp stag-handled bowie knife, with his Colt pistol, and the Spencer rifle he cradled in his arms.

Ruff Justice, gentleman and frontier philosopher—good men respected him, bad men feared him, and women, good and bad, wanted him with all the wildness of the Old West.

1

Outside the little farmhouse it was beginning to snow. Ruff Justice couldn't have cared less. The tall, mustached man was lying naked on his back, the crazy quilt folded down to his waist, his head propped up on a thick pillow. His eyes were busy watching the big, hearty blond woman bustling around the room.

She was naked as well. Naked, merry, healthy, and eager to please.

Her name was Mrs. Cole Cairot, and she was a widow with a small place up in the brakes on the Missouri River above Bismarck, Dakota Territory. She got along well without a man most times, but now and then her healthy widow's body cried out for a male creature, and when she chose one, he was well treated.

"Carrie, don't bring more food. Please," Ruff begged.

"A man has to eat," the blonde said. She crossed the room, her great firm breasts jutting from her relatively slender body. Her stride, her hips, were purposeful and appealing to the eye. She carried a tray of food, steaming food—potatoes and gravy made from the drippings of a rare, juicy roast; slices of that roast and corn cut from the cob and soaked in fresh butter; biscuits and honey; and dark rich coffee made by a woman who knew how to make it.

"A man has just got to eat, Justice."

"I've eaten," he said. "And eaten."

"You go ahead and have a try," Carrie Cairot insisted. She put the tray on Ruff's lap, letting her hand go briefly to his crotch beneath the quilt, rubbing him and encouraging him, urging him to new efforts. She sat on the bed facing him, smiling, and put one of his hands on her sturdy breasts, breasts meant for suckling fat children. There was nothing fragile or delicate about her. She was a strapping, life-loving, giving woman meant for hard work, for cooking and mending, for birthing a calf or chopping wood, for scrubbing a man's back after a hard twelve hours in the field, for getting into bed with him and being rocked on, sucked at, bitten, used, and snuggled to.

Ruff had pretty much done all of that. Carrie had seemed grateful, taking it all with a laugh, a smile of pleasure, a tight hug, and a wet, openmouthed kiss.

"You cut two cords of wood for me, Justice, and dug that well out again. I've got to pay you back some way."

"You have, Carrie. You have done that."

"What, going to bed with you! Why, man, what do you think I got you out here for? I owe you for that. And I'm trying to repay you."

Ruff reached up, took her hair at the base of her neck, and pulled her to him. She came, sighing with pleasure, to meet his kiss. The tray rocked and started to slide, and Carrie sat up.

"Not going to eat?" she asked.

"Later."

"Later," she said, "it'll be cold." But she was already putting the tray aside and folding back the quilt. Crawling in bed with Ruff Justice, she lay on top of him, her lips tasting him, and liking the taste.

Ruff rubbed her back and then let his hands run down to her healthy, firm buttocks, and she spread her thighs, sitting up to ease forward and settle onto Ruff's hard length.

She bent forward so that his lips could reach her pink nipples, could find the valley between her hearty breasts, and she smiled, throwing her head back with pleasure as she stroked against him. Ruff toyed with her body, touching her between the legs where he entered her warmth, caressing those magnificent breasts, her sturdy thighs, and long, smooth back as she swayed and pitched and worked her pelvis against his, taking the business of pleasure very seriously at the moment.

The last thing in the world they needed just then was a rap on the door in the other room. Justice tried very hard to ignore it, as did Carrie, but the knocking was insistent, demanding, and he finally gave it up.

"Better see who it is," Justice said.

"I don't care who it is," she said sleepily. "Let 'em go away."

"That was my idea, but they don't seem to be going."

"They will."

She began to roll and sway against him again, her body rapidly responding to her efforts, turning soft and heavy, slack and warm.

The knocking continued.

"Damn all," Carrie muttered.

That about covered it, Ruff thought. He held her near for another minute, letting his finger trail down the knuckles of her curved spine to its base and then back up again. The knocking persisted.

"That's it," she said. "I'm going to rap on someone's head."

"Might be important."

"Nothing important happens out here, Ruffin. All it can be is someone looking for you."

"No one knows where I am."

"No?" She brightened up a little. "Then maybe I'll just run out and see what it is . . . then we can get back to it." She bit his earlobe lightly and breathed a few sensual words into his ear. Then Carrie slipped from the bed, put on her cotton wrapper, flounced back her hair, and padded to the front door. Ruff lay watching the snowfall outside the window. It was early for snow, but you never knew in Dakota.

Carrie was back.

"It's—" she began, but the man behind her pushed on past before she could finish.

It was Staff Sgt. Wadie Cairot, called "Carrot" because of his name and the shockingly orange head of hair he had under that military cap.

"It's me, scout," Cairot said. His fists were tightly clenched. His mouth was grim and nasty.

"Good," Justice's response was carefully measured. There was anger in his ice-blue eyes for anyone who cared to read it, but Cairot wasn't that perceptive. He was slightly stupid, a little vicious. "Now, why don't you just take yourself on out, Cairot."

"Me, why, you son of a bitch—"

"Easy," Justice warned.

"What the hell are you doing in here?" Cairot demanded.

"Mister Justice was invited to—" Carrie started to tell him.

"Shut up," the NCO said sharply.

"What are *you* doing here, Carrot?" Ruff asked, deliberately using the provocative nickname.

"Me, I got the right. This is my brother's wife!"

"Your brother's dead, Carrot."

"Don't you call me that, damn you."

"Cole's been dead two years, darn you, Wadie Cairot," Carrie snapped.

"That don't make no difference. It still ain't right—my brother's widow sleeping with some tramp like this Justice. I know all about you, scout."

Apparently he didn't, not enough to be wary of the tall man. Ruff Justice had killed his share of men: Indians, white gunmen, and thieves, the few who had had the guts to stand up to him and go at it with guns or knives. Justice had used the big bowie he carried from time to time.

At this moment Justice was ready to tear down Sgt. Wadie Cairot's house, but there was something nearly pathetic about the way Carrot tried to protect his dead brother's wife's honor, and Justice let it pass.

In the next breath Cairot said, "Colonel Mac-Enroe's looking all over blazes for you, Justice."

"So he sent you here?" Carrie asked.

"He sent people out everywhere. I just happened to think where a son of a bitch like Justice would go, and so I—"

That was one time too much. Justice leapt out of bed naked, crossed the room in two strides, and smashed his forearm into Cairot's windpipe. The sergeant's head slammed back against the wall behind him, and Cairot, gurgling, gasping, slid to the floor to sit there, pawing at his flapped holster.

Ruff lifted Cairot's regulation Schofield pistol and ejected the loads. He handed the revolver to Carrie. "Store this somewhere."

"Will he die?" Carrie asked, hunching over her brother-in-law.

"From that, no."

11

"Sorry this had to happen here, Ruffin," Carrie said, rising, leaving Wadie Cairot to his choking and coughing. She put her arms around Justice and hugged him.

"He's not your responsibility. You don't owe me an apology, not at all."

"You won't get in trouble for hitting a sergeant, will you?" she asked with some concern.

"It doesn't work that way with a civilian scout. No, they can't do anything to me. Except fire me, and that would be the best thing that could happen."

"Then you'd come back."

"I'd come back," Ruff Justice said, and she kissed him again, with one of those deep, warm, moist kisses. Only this one meant good-bye. "I've got to pull those stumps today. Six of 'em out back," she said with a sigh.

"Carrie, why don't you get yourself a steady man?"

"Why?" She laughed. "What's wrong with this setup?" Still, it seemed there was a little sadness behind her smile. She kissed Justice again, briefly, and went off to dress.

Justice did the same as Wadie Cairot sat on the floor, glaring at him with tiny malevolent eyes.

Justice dressed slowly, putting on his fringed buckskin shirt, his buckskin pants, and the gun belt with the long-barreled Colt hanging on the right side, the stag-handled bowie knife dangling in back. Inside his fringed boot was a small, razor-edged skinning knife. When he finished brushing his long dark hair, which flowed over his shoulders, he put on a new white stetson hat with a yellow woman's scarf tied around it for a hatband.

In the corner stood a big .56 Spencer repeating rifle in a beaded buckskin sheath. Ruff Justice gathered that into his arms like a mother cradling its child, its too deadly child, and then he walked to Cairot.

"Ready to go?"

"Damn you, you—"

"Don't say it," Justice warned him with a smile, and Cairot, who had already had one taste of Ruff Justice, decided to take that good advice. He got to his feet and stood there, befuddled, angry, looking around the room.

"Where in hell's my pistol?" he asked, patting his empty holster.

"Don't know. You don't need it."

"What am I supposed to tell Supply?"

"Use your imagination. You've proven you've got a good one."

"What do you mean?"

"You found me, didn't you?"

"I found you, and if I'd had any sense, I would have come in here without knocking, come in with that Schofield in my hand . . . Maybe next time I will," he muttered.

"You're not threatening me, are you, Cairot?"

"No." Wadie Cairot rubbed his throat. It felt like something was broken in there. "I'm not threatening you, Justice."

His eyes shuttled away, and Justice knew he had a dangerous man here. Wadie Cairot was one of those who couldn't stand up face to face with Justice, but he couldn't forgive, either. That left only one option: a bullet in the back from an ambush, a knife across the throat as Ruff slept. Justice had made an enemy, a deadly one. He could only hope that whatever assignment Col. MacEnroe had for him, wherever he was going, Wadie Cairot wasn't going to be with him.

"He doesn't mean anything," Carrie told him as

they went out the door into the snowy day. The oaks along the river were stark and gray against the white background.

"He doesn't?" Ruff asked.

"He was close to Cole, real close, that's all. Wadie found this place for us, Ruffin. He used to come out to Sunday supper all the time. Then, when that rattler put Cole down, Wadie kind of got lost and maybe even went a little crazy."

A little crazy—that was it. That was the light dancing in Sgt. Cairot's eyes that Justice hadn't quite put a name to. It was madness, a killing madness.

And now that madness had found a target. Ruff swung aboard his big black horse, bent low, kissed Carrie good-bye, and rode out toward Fort Abraham Lincoln in the lightly falling, damp snow.

And he could feel them on his back, could feel the mad little eyes boring holes in him as Wadie Cairot watched the tall, buckskin-clad scout ride from the little snow-dusted ranch in the Missouri Brakes.

2

Mack Pierce was a massive bear of a man. As first sergeant of Fort Abraham Lincoln, Dakota Territory, Pierce made it a rule not to move quickly—not to move at all unless it was necessary. His three-hundred-plus pounds took some moving, and little aside from the commanding officer's bark could bring him to his feet.

He came to his feet now as Ruff Justice entered the orderly room. "Ruffin! Where have you been and what have you been doing?"

"Taking a few days' leave, Mack, that's all." Ruff sat on the corner of Pierce's desk and the big sergeant shook his head sadly.

"A few days' leave—you should have seen Wadie Cairot storm through here."

"Wadie Cairot worries about a lot of things that aren't his business, Mack."

"You're probably right there, but all I know is what I see of Carrot on the post. He's a good soldier, Ruffin."

"He ought to stick to the soldiering then and lay off the preaching—he hasn't got the knack for it." Ruff raised his eyes toward the commanding officer's door. "What's up?"

"You won't like it is what's up," Pierce said, sagging back into his chair.

"That's pretty definite." Justice grinned.

"I'm going to let the colonel fill you in, Ruffin. I'll just say this: you won't be grinning like that when you come out of his office."

"Like that, do you mean . . . ?"

The door to the colonel's office opened and MacEnroe himself stuck his head out to look into the orderly room. When he saw Justice, his eyes narrowed and he inclined his head. "Come in, Justice."

Ruff didn't like the tone of Col. MacEnroe's voice. MacEnroe was unhappy. That meant that Mack Pierce was right: whatever this assignment was, Justice wasn't going to find it to his liking. He tossed his hat at the hat tree in the corner, missed, and went into the office.

Col. MacEnroe wasn't alone. There were four others in the office. A blonde wearing yellow and black and a coolly amused smile sat beside the colonel's desk. She met Ruff's gaze with curious green eyes.

In time Ruff was able to tear his eyes from the blond woman's sleek beauty to have a look at the others. He was introduced.

"Ruff, this is Sir Henry Landis," MacEnroe told him. A tall Britisher with a perfectly waxed black mustache and flat, pale eyes nodded a bare inch and got much the same response from Justice.

MacEnroe tried again. "This is his brother, Sir Oswald Tyler Landis."

Oswald was a shorter, stouter version of Henry. His hair was thinner, more brown than jet black. He stuck out a hand and said something that sounded like, "Chadoo."

"This is Lady Celia, Sir Henry's wife," MacEnroe

went on, seeming to place unusual emphasis on the last word. The blonde's smile deepened.

Ruff stepped toward her, took her hand, and kissed it gently between two knuckles.

Sir Oswald mumbled something like, "I say!" His brother said nothing but continued to glower darkly. His eyes measured Ruff and seemed to find nothing challenging about the tall plainsman. The fourth person in the office interrupted the brief moment of tension.

"Is anyone going to introduce me, or am I not important enough to worry about?"

There was a pleasant tone of self-mockery in the voice, and Justice turned to see a very pretty young woman in twill. She was American by the accent, blue-eyed, her reddish-brown hair pinned tightly to her skull. She looked like a schoolteacher or maybe a bank teller.

"Miss Laura York," the colonel said. The expression in his eyes was still not a happy one, Ruff noticed. The colonel was a fighting man, a soldier, but he was no diplomat. He got a little antsy when civilian visitors showed up at Lincoln, disrupting his post routine. "Miss York is a reporter," the colonel said, nearly choking on the word. MacEnroe had no use for reporters—they either glorified the military or attacked it unnecessarily. Custer's experiences with the press provided an unhappy precedent.

"A woman reporter," Justice said, mulling the idea over. It was the first time he had run into such a creature.

"Does it bother you that I'm a woman?" Laura York demanded.

"Not yet. Give it time," Ruff answered.

Lady Celia smiled again, Sir Oswald swallowed a guffaw. Laura was clearly not amused.

17

The colonel pressed on. "Sit down, Ruffin. We've got a project here that might interest you."

Which meant that the colonel had something by the tail that he wanted badly to let go of. Justice took a seat and waited to hear what the colonel had on his mind. It took MacEnroe a moment to sort out his thoughts—that was fine with Ruff Justice. He used the time to good advantage, studying the lines of Lady Celia's body. She had a way of positioning herself that, taken bit by bit, was perfectly proper, but as a whole was entirely sexual and intriguing. Ruff Justice was intrigued.

"You may have heard of Sir Henry," the colonel said, "certainly his reputation is well-known, worldwide in fact."

"I haven't heard," Ruff said. Henry shot him a scathing glance. "But then we don't see or hear much out here."

"No." The colonel tried to warn Ruff with a glance, but Justice refused to meet his gaze. His eyes were busy.

"Sir Henry is a sportsman, Ruff," the colonel went on. "He has spent a total of three years in Africa, two in India hunting trophies. He has been to the Orient and to Russia, taking everything from yak to elephant, bear to reindeer, tiger, and rhinoceros. But this is his first safari to the western United States . . ."

"A hunter?" Ruff Justice asked.

"Why, yes."

"Sir, with Stone Eyes out there, it's hardly the time for a pleasure excursion, is it?"

"Ruffin, would you like to see the letter from the Secretary of the Interior that requests that Sir Henry be given all possible assistance?"

"No." Justice just shook his head. He was in silent sympathy with the colonel. MacEnroe knew the situation on the plains better than anyone. He knew that Stone Eyes, a renegade Sioux, was out there letting blood, knew that there had been reports of Jack Cavanaugh's gang raiding settlers' wagon trains and the small outposts, and that Cavanaugh, an unreconstructed rebel, was reputed to be as bad or worse than Stone Eyes.

It was no time to be strolling the plains looking for big-game trophies.

The colonel, however, was army. He did what he was told to do. He didn't have to like it. This Sir Henry Landis obviously had some pull somewhere in Washington. What he wanted, he got. It didn't mean he was smart. A smart man would have listened to the advice MacEnroe had undoubtedly already given him.

A smart man wouldn't take a beautiful young wife out with him on the prairie.

"Buffalo," Sir Oswald began, apparently without provocation. "Great bull buffalo and grizzly. Mountain lion and elk. Or do you call them wapiti? Antelope and moose—we will find moose?" he asked Justice.

"I've no idea what you'll find, other than trouble," Justice said soberly.

"What do you mean?"

"I mean, you're crazy if you go, I'm crazy if I agree to guide you. There are other hunters out there, you know, Sir Henry. Death hunters."

"Red Indians, you mean. We hardly have to worry about them. We're taking twelve wagons, Justice. Twelve wagons, over one hundred weapons, and thirty-seven able men."

"Custer," Ruff Justice told them, "had two hundred and sixty-one."

"Then you refuse to guide us?" Sir Henry asked.

He was incredulous. Where he came from men didn't refuse their lord anything.

"The colonel has assured us that he will do his best to protect us from the Indians," Sir Henry said as if it were all a joke. "A cavalry patrol is going along with us. Does that calm your fears, Mister Justice?"

"Sure. It doesn't make the whole idea much smarter, though."

Sir Henry stiffened and paled a little. Laura York spoke up. "Is this the Ruff Justice we've heard about all the way to Minneapolis? Why, I thought you were fearless and bold, a true plainsman."

"Did you?"

"Why, yes. It's one reason I wanted to come along on this expedition. Of course I was fascinated by the opportunity to meet and travel with Lord and Lady Landis, but I have to admit I wanted to interview you, Justice. Why, there's just got to be a story in you."

Ruff didn't answer her directly. He had run into a few reporters, too, though none of the female sex, and they had generally done their damnedest to make him look like either a fool or a hero. Justice didn't figure himself for either.

"Well," Sir Henry said, taking his wife's elbow and helping her from the chair, "I'm sure I don't have the time to stand around and try to coerce Mister Justice into guiding us. I'll leave that to you, Colonel MacEnroe. I must say that I am at best indifferent to the entire matter. I have a rough country scout of my own with me, as you know."

"Yes, I do know, but Honus Hall is hardly the man I'd choose to guide you on the plains," the colonel said. Ruff Justice would have put it more strongly. His eyebrow lifted and he pushed his lip out thoughtfully.

Honus Hall knew the country, all right, but old Honus was an out-and-out scoundrel. You wouldn't want to lie down beside Honus if he had a knife or a rock. You might not get up again. He had done some shady work but had somehow managed to avoid the hangman. His luck couldn't last forever. Ruff looked at Lady Celia and shook his head.

He didn't much like the idea of Honus Hall being in charge of her fate. Justice stepped aside to let the English party by. Sir Henry's pale eyes swept past Ruff as if trying not to see him. His lady was another matter. She saw him, and by the quick little uplift at the corners of her mouth, she liked what she saw.

The redheaded reporter saw it all, and whether she liked it or not, she was certainly tucking it away in some compartment of her mind for possible future use.

Sir Oswald gave Justice his limp hand again and then went out, closing the door behind him. Ruff was left alone with Col. MacEnroe.

With an audible, hoarse sigh, MacEnroe sagged into his chair, ripped open his bottom drawer, and removed the bottle of whiskey he kept there.

"Sometimes I envy you, Justice."

"Sir?"

"You say pretty much what you want to say."

"Not always."

The colonel looked at the whiskey in his glass and downed it quickly, as if it were medicine. "This Landis—too many top connections. Friend of Senator Ghostly and of the Secretary of the Interior. What the hell am I supposed to do when he shows up with this idiotic request, tell him what I think of it?"

The colonel started to put his bottle away, changed his mind, and had another short one.

"Well?" he asked Ruff Justice.

"I don't like this, sir."

"But you'll guide them? It's you or Honus Hall."

"That's another question—where did they pick up Hall and why did he attach himself to Sir Henry?"

"That's obvious, isn't it? Money. The lord has to be loaded—any man who's spent the better part of the last five years going around the world shooting whatever moves has to have money."

"And what does the Lady Landis think about all this? Is he ever home?"

"You'd have to ask her," the colonel said.

"Who's leading the patrol you're sending out with the lord and his lady, sir?"

"Who? Sergeant Cairot."

"Carrot!"

"I'm short again, Ruffin. Hardistein is down on the Cannonball with Lieutenant Wailing. Lieutenant Greer is home on leave. Sergeant Mullins still has that bad knee. Who am I going to send, Mack Pierce?" The colonel looked at Ruff more closely. "Are you and Cairot having trouble of some kind, Justice?"

"Only a little."

"Not enough to stop you from doing this job for me?"

"No, sir, I expect not, only I've spent some time on the river."

The colonel didn't understand. "Yes?" he prompted.

"On the riverboats, sir."

They didn't seem to be getting any closer. "I don't get you, Ruffin."

"It's just this, sir. Any riverboat gambler would give his eyeteeth to be able to stack a deck like the one you've dealt me."

It didn't shape up real well. An arrogant English lord and his proud lady. That was a pair, all right. Throw in Wadie Cairot, who wanted Justice's blood, and Honus Hall as a wild card. Then there were Stone Eyes and the bandit Jack Cavanaugh waiting out on the plains to pick up the pot. And any mistake Ruff or the colonel made was liable to find its way into print via the redheaded lady reporter. Too many jokers.

"You'll do it, Justice?"

"Yes, sir," Ruff Justice answered. "Damned if I know why, but I'll take the lord a-hunting."

Maybe he did know why he was going to take on this job. The reason had pale hair and green eyes and the catlike logic of a woman on the prowl. Maybe Lady Celia was married, but she didn't look much like she wanted to stay that way.

She looked like fair game.

Ruff left the colonel in his office and went out into the orderly room. Pierce looked up and winked. The man knew everything that happened on that post before it happened. Ruff gave him a mock scowl, snatched up his hat, and went out into the brilliant sunlight.

He stood for a while on the plank walk in front of the headquarters building watching the soldiers drill, the flag waving in the light breeze. He had been away from Fort Lincoln for quite some time.

It looked like they figured on making it quite a homecoming.

3

Their camp was across the Missouri River. They hadn't even tried to fit into the fort's confines. Not with twelve wagons and nearly forty people. It was a fine and fancy outfit, and just looking at it, Ruff knew there was going to be a problem. The wagons, freshly painted, were too light by half. Three of them were enclosed and painted with gold curlicues, with a coat of arms on each.

The camp hands looked as though they'd been dredged up from everywhere on earth.

A few of them looked to be English gentlemen, barbered and shaved, wearing dark suits and derby hats. Others were the unshaven, tobacco-jowled hands you could pick up on any western street—or in the saloons.

Ruff recognized a man here and there. Some of them didn't seem too happy to be recognized—like Sam Cukor, who had gotten drunk one night and decided to take Ruff's head off with a fire ax. Sam had gotten himself a broken arm out of that.

Ruff still had his head.

"Justice!" A familiar voice called from the sunlit cottonwood trees that stood in rustling ranks along the river.

"Hawk!" Ruff answered with genuine pleasure,

turning the big black horse he had bought from Ezra Stevens in the direction of the voice.

Hawk was an Arikara Indian, a member of a tribe that was already virtually extinct. The great raiding tribes—the Sioux, Cheyenne, and Pawnee—had nearly wiped out the smaller tribe, which from time's beginning had its home on the Upper Missouri.

His real name was Where the Lone Hawk Flies, but the Arik word was virtually unpronounceable for a white tongue, and Hawk simplified everything.

Hawk knew the river and he knew the plains. He knew the Sioux and detested them. There were two fingers cut off his right hand, one for his wife, one for his only son. Both killed by Teton Dakotas.

"Hello, Hawk," Ruff said, swinging down from his horse. "What are you doing with this lacy outfit?"

They shook hands warmly. Hawk answered with a grin, "It's a month's pay, maybe more if it don't snow. Honus Hall brought me on. I'll be doing the skinning."

"Honus." Ruff's expression turned dark.

"Yes, I know—dirty man—but when you got to work, what do you care who the boss is? Good money, Justice. You? The army sends you?"

"Yes, though with an army patrol and a good guide like you, I don't know what I'm needed for."

"Maybe to watch the white women?" Hawk asked.

"They might take some watching. Damn, don't these people believe what they hear?"

"Stone Eyes?" Hawk's expression was briefly clouded by anger, tribal hatred. He shrugged. "They don't know nothin', Ruff. City people from somewhere East—England or something like that."

"I saw old Sam Cukor. Anyone else we know riding with this outfit, Hawk?"

"No one I know. But some white men I don't know who looked very bad to me."

"What do you mean, 'bad?'"

"Look like they want to shoot somebody, Ruffin T. Me, anyone. I stay away from 'em. Figure they might want to try shooting Indians and practice on an old Arik." Hawk laughed, shook his head, and said, "You'll see them pretty quick. You'll see what I mean."

Ruff figured he would see them soon enough, but he wondered what they were there for—they had to be gunmen of some kind from Hawk's perceptive description. Not hunters or plainsmen, for Hawk would have seen the long plains, the mountains, and skies in their eyes and known them for what they were. These were men who practiced the fast draw, burning up hundreds of rounds of ammunition in the hope of getting a chance at the real thing—a chance to kill.

Kill who? Justice wondered.

"Army's coming over," Hawk said, pointing southward toward the river ford. Sure enough, there came Carrot's patrol—all twelve of them. Hardly enough to keep Stone Eyes awake nights worrying.

"What do you think of all this?" Justice asked. "It seems like a lot of money and effort for a few trophies, doesn't it?"

"What do I think?" The Arik shrugged. "Most whites are crazy anyway. They pay me, let them be crazy."

Justice swung aboard the black gelding again and rode into the camp proper, where everyone, Sir Henry and his lady included, had turned out to meet the cavalry patrol.

Looking wary and sober, Cairot left his men as they reached the camp perimeter and came forward alone, walking his bay into the circle of wagons. He saluted Sir Henry and swung down.

"Colonel MacEnroe's compliments, sir," Cairot said stiffly. He was obviously a little awed by Sir Henry. He wasn't the least bit awed by Ruff Justice, however. The sergeant let his eyes flicker to Ruff's briefly and the glance he gave Justice told him that he hadn't forgotten. He was still going to get Justice as soon as the opportunity presented itself.

Or try to, anyway.

"I want to get moving right away," Sir Henry said. His manner was abrupt. He expected no response and got none, except for the bobbing of Cairot's head. "I've instructed my people to begin readying the wagons. I expect we shall be ready in half an hour."

Leaning against a wagon wheel with his arms crossed, Justice held the reins to the big black horse and watched them. Cairot spun away as Sir Henrys' own people got to work, harnessing the teams, packing the wagons.

Justice saw the lean man with the red beard and he walked toward him, leading his horse. Sir Henry's retinue surrounded him, swearing and running and sweating hard.

Honus Hall looked like he was holding a full house or better. He smiled at Justice in his old, smug way as Ruff came up to where the scoundrel stood beneath a big oak tree.

"Howdy, Justice," Hall said. He turned his head and spat out a stream of tobacco juice. "How's things?"

"They smell, Honus."

"Yeah?" Hall laughed. He stroked his red beard, lifted his eyes briefly to the sounds of shouting—

27

someone had lost a horse—and then looked again at Justice. "What makes you say a thing like that, Justice?"

"You."

Honus Hall stiffened. "Does that mean something?"

"It means you smell," Ruff said flatly. "And anywhere I find you, something dirty must be up. Why don't you just leave now, Honus, before something happens to you?"

"Threats? The army pays you to threaten honest citizens, Justice?" Hall laughed again, dryly. "Hell, no, I'm not leaving. Why don't you pull up stakes? We've got me, the Arik, a dozen cavalrymen, and the lord's men. What the hell do we need with one more two-bit scout?"

He had a point there, Justice thought privately. To Hall he said, "The others don't know you as well as I do. The colonel thought someone ought to be along to keep an eye on you. And I mean to."

"Yeah," Hall said mockingly, "keep an eye on me. Watch me till you've got eye strain. What do I care? It's just a little scouting job. I took it when Landis offered it. Why do you want to make a crime out of it?"

"I don't," Justice said. "Do you?"

Hall mumbled a curse and Justice swung aboard the black gelding, still watching him—it didn't do to turn your back on Honus Hall.

"You might turn back, Honus," Justice said again. "You just might save yourself some trouble and turn back."

"Screw yourself, Justice," Hall said, but he said it quietly and Ruff let him think he hadn't heard him. Hall knew. He knew Justice could take him apart piece by piece. He just liked to pretend to himself that it wasn't so.

28

Hall had killed, would kill again. He had guided three rich Easterners into the Big Horns five years ago. It had been a hard winter, a very hard winter. Only Honus Hall had come back out of those mountains. The others, he said, had died from exposure.

For months after that Honus Hall had spent money like it was water. He was that kind of man. Justice kneed the black, which took one rebellious sidestep, hunched its back, and then straightened, loping out onto the long plains while behind Justice the ponderous wagon train tried to get itself into motion.

The whole thing smelled.

He told himself that as he rode. The smell of it nearly filled his nostrils, forcing away the good clean smells of long grass and cool air, sage and greasewood. After a mile the wagons had become mere dots on the plains. The Missouri itself was only a silver thread, Bismarck a few scattered cubes. But the smell lingered on.

Ruff slowed the horse to a walk. When they finally got rolling, the wagons would have to follow the trail Ruff now rode. They needed no guiding, or no more than Honus Hall and Carrot could give them. Ruff's job was to find game to kill, to find the Indians before they could kill Sir Henry.

It was bound to be interesting.

The lady who came riding toward him promised to make it even more interesting. She wore a green velvet divided riding skirt and matching jacket, and a black cap that allowed her yellow hair to stream out behind her as she rode. She straddled a long-legged buckskin horse with a creamy tail and mane. Her cheeks were red with the exertion, with the kiss of the cold wind.

"Hello there," she said as if she hadn't expected

to find Justice there at all. Her voice was lying, but her eyes spoke the truth: she had known he would be there, had come looking for him.

"Hello, Lady Celia."

"Lady Celia." She laughed. "Just Celia, please."

"And I'll just call your husband Henry," Ruff said. "I'm sure he'd appreciate that little familiarity."

"Oh, Henry . . ." She waved a hand in the air. Her breath was still coming in spurts and gasps—she must have been riding very hard indeed. "His way of looking at things is a little different."

"Than yours? Or mine?"

"Than anyone's. I never have called him Sir Henry or Lord Landis or anything at all like that, not even in the days before we were married, when I was just a long-legged dancer down on Toynbee Street."

"A dancer? You don't mean that."

She laughed again. "Sure I do. Now, then, don't you believe everything I tell you, Mister Ruffin Justice?" Her accent now was heavily Irish with perhaps a shadow of cockney. "Sound different?" she asked, regaining her refined tones.

"You were a commoner."

"The commonest," she said with a laugh, and her green eyes danced.

"But he married you."

"Sure. The lord had eyes for long legs." She was thoughtful for a moment. "Ale and champagne and hot blood—well, he wanted me to sleep with him and I held out and look at me now, lady of the manor."

"Yes—well?"

"Well, what?" she responded.

"Was it worth it?" Ruff Justice asked.

"Hell, yes." She smiled. "Coarse, ain't I? It was

worth it. Have you ever seen poverty, Justice, real poverty, big-city poverty?"

"Briefly." He had seen it and it was dirty. Out here a man could be hungry and still have pride. He could hunt or forage or till the earth. He could work and the cool evening winds would chill his sweat-soaked body and he could put aside his tools and know that he had done his best, that he was poor but building, doing with what he had, hoping for better times.

In the cities Ruff had seen it had been different. On the tours he had made east with Cody reading his slapdash poetry to people who seemed anxious to hear it, to hear anything fresh and clean and hopeful—virile—out of the West, he had seen them. Dark-eyed, watching from buildings that were young but already decaying, already dirty. No matter what their age, they looked like people hope has fled from. It shouldn't be that way, Ruff knew. Had the cities made the people that way, or had the people made the cities?

"He taught me how to speak, to dress, to behave. It really didn't matter," Lady Celia said, "his friends and family knew what I was."

"A dancer."

"A commoner. They still place a lot of weight on class, Justice."

"Yes." Justice knew it was so. He had met some of them in Europe the time he and Buffalo Bill had made that circuit. He had also met a few of the higher-class women who wanted a little of that Western virility. "How did you handle it?" he asked.

"*Henry* handled it by being absent," Celia told him. "God, year after year he was gone hunting this, that, or the other. How many elephants can you shoot? I suppose he was hiding out."

"You stayed home."

"If you can call the castle home. Yes"—she smiled—"a real castle. Fifteenth century. Moat and battlements, a small dungeon—very small. Henry's ancestors were civilized, apparently. I stayed home," she sighed, "with the relatives and the family retainers and the gentry and the townspeople, with the boredom and the gossip and the whispering behind hands everywhere I went. They did pity the good lord so."

"This time you came along."

They parted briefly as they rode through a sudden, deep coulee gashed into the plains. Down the sandy slope and up the far side they rode, the horses laboring, spraying sand into the air.

"I came along," Lady Celia said when they could talk again, "because it had to be better than sitting alone in a fifty-two-blinkin'-stone house waiting for something, anything, that never seemed to happen."

Ruff nodded. It was a story he might have heard a hundred times before. "How's it been? The hunting trip to America?" he asked.

Lady Celia had been expecting something different, sympathy maybe. Ruff didn't have a lot to give her. She had tried to take a great leap upward. She had married a man far above her, a man whose world she didn't understand. She had paid a price but she had gotten what she went after. He couldn't give her much sympathy; in life you give a little to gain a little.

"It's been more fun than anything that's happened for years," she said.

"You're getting along with your husband?"

She shook her head. "He doesn't want me here."

"Why?"

"How would I know? I'm a reminder of his folly, I suppose."

"I'd think he'd be proud of you," Ruff Justice said, and it wasn't an unprovoked compliment. She was woman, all woman, and a man who cared if she knew which fork to use first didn't deserve her.

"Well, maybe . . ." Her thoughts, her eyes drifted away briefly, looking to the skies, where a few white clouds stained the deep blue of the day. "Is that where we're going?" she asked, pointing toward the distant, low mountains.

"I hope not."

"What do you mean?"

"That's Stone Eyes' stronghold," Ruff told her.

"Is he very cruel?"

Justice told her straight out. "You wouldn't believe it, lady."

"But why? Is it because the white man has treated him so badly?"

Ruff laughed. "Sure."

"Why are you laughing at me?"

"I'm not," Justice said more seriously. "It's just that people get ideas."

"Such as?"

"Such as the Indian living in peaceful contentment before the white man came, when the fact is the Indian's life has always been constant warfare. The life of all human beings has always been just that. Some win, some lose. It's numbers or technology that makes the difference. If the Indians had either of those, they would have won, would have eliminated us, and maybe someday some Indian historian would tell us how the whites, who only wanted to farm on the land, were killed by the warlike Sioux and Cheyenne."

"You don't like them at all, do you?"

"The Indians?"

"You don't sound like it."

"Hell, yes, I like them. I like them a hell of a lot

more than people who sit around feeling sorry for them or glorifying them, telling stories that only make the Indian into a white man so we can understand him—these dime-novel fellahs. I like the Indian for what he is: brave and strong and willing to live without being coddled, to stand up to nature and his enemies ... And I'll tell you one thing more: I've known plenty of them, more than many after me will know, and the Indian is a laughing, giving man, a loving woman ..." Ruff's tirade broke off into muttered syllables.

Lady Celia nodded wisely and asked, "Who was she? This Indian woman."

"I don't know," Ruff said, "what the hell you're talking about."

She had an answer for him. It formed itself on her lips, but the sound of the bullet whipping past their heads wiped it away. Justice heard the rifle shot echoing across the plains and then he was leaping from the back of his black horse, his body meeting Lady Celia's, and then they were falling as the death guns spoke.

4

They hit the ground hard, Justice rolling with the woman as the distant gun roared again. A wash no more than two feet deep was carved into the plains, and into it Justice dragged and rolled the lady, her green eyes wide with fear and astonishment.

Justice pressed her to the earth, her body against his, her eyes looking up at him in silent amazement. Ruff's big .56 Spencer had been lost in the fall, but he had his long-barreled Colt in his hand. His eyes searched the horizon for the smoke from the last shot, smoke that the wind now rapidly whipped away . . . that and nothing else. He still didn't move. He lay there with the woman beneath him and the Colt in hand, his thumb wrapped around its curved hammer, watching, waiting.

"What is it . . . who?" Lady Celia panted. "Is it the Indians?"

"No. Not this close to Lincoln."

"But it must be! The robbers then—this Cavanaugh and his men."

Justice shook his head. Jack Cavanaugh didn't work that way. Jack was evil and had as much right to exist as a rabid wolf, but he wouldn't snipe at someone and then run down to strip the bodies of any valuables. He would know that the shots could bring others from the wagon train. Jack was slime but no one had said he was stupid.

"Then it was . . ." She broke off. Justice's eyes flickered to her face—it was pale and strained.

"I don't know who it was, lady."

"They want to kill me."

"Who does?"

But she shook her head, and that was that. She would say no more. Justice could see the horsemen coming now, men from the Landis party. Their horses kicked up tiny puffs of yellow dust as they ran.

"Help is on the way," Justice said with some irony.

"Henry?" she asked.

"I don't know. No. Don't get up yet. We're as good a target as we were a minute ago."

"But he'll have ridden off," she insisted.

"Who? Who will have ridden off?"

She wouldn't answer. Justice could get no more out of her. Someone wanted to kill the lady? For what reason? Justice figured there was a much better chance that it was someone who had wanted to kill him. There were a few with this outfit who had made their feelings known, a few who just sheltered a silent wish.

Honus Hall, Cairot, Sam Cukor.

And the lord. Something about Justice rubbed Sir Henry the wrong way. He wasn't sure what, but it was a fact. It didn't seem to be a killing grudge, however.

Hell, maybe he was wrong. Maybe it was a lone Sioux or one of Cavanaugh's boys hoping for an extra payday. Maybe.

They rose as the four horsemen rode up and reined in through a storm of dust. Hawk was there, and three men Justice didn't know. Two were apparently English, the other a hire-on skinner from Bismarck.

"What's going on out here?" Hawk asked.

"The Fourth of July. Early." Ruff dusted himself off and looked around for his hat and rifle. He found both and planted his hat, wiping back his long dark hair.

The lady's hat had been trampled by the horses and lay, small and twisted, against the stubbled plains. She just stood there, looking with amazement at the low knolls to the south, the knolls that had sheltered a killer.

"Want us to go look for him, Justice?" Hawk asked, lifting his chin in the direction of the knolls.

"No. He's gone now."

Hawk shrugged. He wasn't getting paid enough to want to go chasing a sniper. A sniper who was very good indeed. It was only now that Hawk saw the bullet hole in the crown of Ruff's hat.

"You live lucky, Justice."

"Think so?"

"Yes, but who knows how long it'll last?"

Ruff smiled thinly. "Who knows?"

He collected the reins to his black horse and swung aboard. No one spoke on the way back, but once when Justice glanced at Lady Celia, her eyes communicated plainly that she thought the bullets had been meant for her. Ruff didn't try to probe her reasons, not then, not with so many ears around them, but it gave him food for thought.

The lord met them a quarter of a mile in front of the slowly rolling wagon train.

He looked more furious than concerned when he arrived, and Justice thought he might have ridden a lot farther than just from the wagon. From the knolls? The lord reined up violently.

"What in hell's going on here? What's happened?

Celia?" He looked at his disheveled and dusty wife and then at Ruff, who was in much the same condition.

Justice spoke up. "Someone took a couple of shots at us out there."

"At you?" Sir Henry demanded the details and Ruff supplied them as best he could. "I can't understand this," he said when Justice had finished. "And just what were you and Lady Celia doing together out there in the first place?"

"I was riding. She was riding. We met and talked," Justice explained tersely. The lord didn't like it, but then he wasn't really listening. He was glowering at Justice and his wife, believing he already knew what was up.

They were nearly at the wagons when the redheaded lady reporter rode toward them, whipping her dun pony with the reins. She pulled up sharply and turned back beside Justice.

"What is it?" Laura York asked. "What's happening?"

Ruff didn't feel like telling it again. Especially not to a newspaperwoman. "Nothing of much interest."

"Oh, come now," she said insistently.

"I fell off my horse. These folks picked me up."

Hawk laughed out loud.

Crimson spots appeared on Laura York's cheeks. "Is that supposed to be funny?"

"I don't know. Print it and see if it gets a laugh."

"I'd like to print it. With the same sneering intonation. Do you think I'm amusing, Mister Justice? Is it funny that I'm a woman doing a man's job?"

"There's nothing at all funny about you," Justice said.

"The more I learn about you, the less I like you, Justice. Keep talking. I'll have the truth about you in every paper between here and Denver."

"God," he moaned, "not the *truth*."

The lady had completely run out of tolerance. With a knifelike glance at Justice she heeled her horse and it leapt forward, leaving the rest of them behind.

"You're cruel, Justice," Lady Celia said.

"Am I? I'll apologize to her. I thought she could take a little ribbing, a tough newspaperman like that."

"Apparently," Sir Henry said dryly, "Miss York shares the common view that Justice is not all that amusing, nor all that interesting."

"Interesting?" Lady Celia said, and she looked Justice up and down again in that slow, intense way of hers. "Now, that is the wrong word, Henry. He is definitely very *interesting*."

Surprising them all, Sir Henry laughed. He threw back his head and laughed. When he was done, he told Justice, "We dine at seven," and slapping his big roan with his quirt, he raced away.

"Was that an invitation?" Justice asked the lady.

"That," she said, looking him over again, "is just what that was. An invitation."

Then she too was gone and Justice, frowning, was left to ride in with Hawk and the remaining men.

"You see," the Arik said. "That's why the colonel sent you—to make plenty of friends for him."

"It looks like it. Hawk, am I missing something or are half these people crazy?"

"Told you before, Ruffin Justice, told you before—all whites are crazy. If you don't understand them, don't ask old Hawk. What do I know?"

Justice swung in toward the wagons and spent some time talking to Pvt. Billy Sondberg. Ruff had done him a sort of favor once—he'd kept him from going before a firing squad.

"How's Carrot?" Ruff asked the kid.

"Well, you know." Sondberg shrugged. "He's moody. That's Carrot for you, though. I've had worse sergeants."

"And a few better."

Billy looked around. The wind folded the brim of his hat back. His eyes twinkled as he answered. "Quite a few better—but you know, Ruffin, it don't do a man any good to complain in the army. Just gets inside you and sort of knots up. It's better to take what they dish out, and if you don't like it, go down the road when your enlistment's up."

"Where is Cairot, Billy?"

"Well, now . . ." Sondberg looked around him and shrugged. "I guess I haven't seen him for a time, come to think of it."

"For how long a time?"

"I don't know. Is it important?"

"Maybe."

The kid pursed his lips. "Maybe an hour."

An hour was just about long enough. "Thanks, Billy."

"For what? Did I help you any, Ruffin?"

"Maybe."

"Say, Justice," Sondberg called before Ruff was out of earshot. "You mind telling me just what in hell this English lord is doing out here with his fancy wagons and fancy guns while Stone Eyes is prowling?"

"I don't mind—but I can't. All good fun and adventure, I guess."

"Yeah," Sondberg called back. "Good fun getting yourself scalped."

"It doesn't do any good," Ruff quoted, "to complain in the army."

Sondberg grinned but his expression quickly faded. Billy was no fool. He knew what sort of a chance they were taking riding out on the plains with a force their size. But civilian pressure had been brought to bear against Col. MacEnroe and so they followed orders on down the line. And if Sir Henry's party happened to be hit by Stone Eyes with his more than a hundred Sioux warriors, well, then, MacEnroe would get the blame.

Ruff had ridden off alone and now he watched the wagons jolt by on a parallel track, the red-faced soldiers and grim civilians stirring up dust. Then he shook his head and lifted his eyes to the horizon. They would be all right tonight—the fort and Bismarck were still too near. Maybe tomorrow night as well.

From then on, they would be nothing but targets.

"Hey! Hey, Justice."

Ruff turned his head slowly, recognizing Laura York's voice, not all that sure he wanted to talk with her again so soon. She rode up beside him and stuck out a hand.

"Friends?" She smiled; it was a nice smile and Ruff took her small hand in his own.

"Sure. Why not?"

"Why not?" she agreed. She wore a flat-crowned hat and a dark-brown riding skirt, with a white blouse that molded itself to her breasts nicely as the wind from the plains drifted over them. "I made a fool of myself earlier."

"That? It was nothing," Justice said. "I'd forgotten it already."

"You're a forgiving man, are you?" she asked brightly.

"Most times."

"I've heard differently," the newspaperwoman said.

"Stories?"

"Stories, yes. True stories. When firsthand

accounts all agree with each other, I think the stories deserve to be called facts. There was something about a man called Tug Slaussen. How many hundreds of miles did you trail him before you killed him, Mister Justice?"

"I don't talk over old fights," Justice said sharply. There was something behind the anger in his blue eyes, something like pain. But Laura had expected that—she already knew the reason behind the Slaussen killing. A woman had been murdered, a good woman, a close friend of Ruff's. "Let the dead lay."

"We were talking about forgiving, Justice," Laura persisted.

"Forgiving . . . sure. I forgive a sharp word, a hard look. I'll forget a fistfight. But not blood. I don't forgive or forget a man who comes to do murder, or does it, or wants to hurt for the fun of it. No, I don't forgive or forget any of those."

"Neither do I, Justice," said Laura York.

Ruff's eyes narrowed still more as he studied the redhead. "What are you talking about?"

"Just who do you think the sniper was trying to kill out there, Justice?"

"Me."

"I don't think so. I think he was trying to kill the woman with you."

"Lady Celia . . ."

"Not Lady Celia. I think he thought it was me. I think it was me your sniper wanted to kill, Mister Justice."

"You?" Ruff half-smiled, but there was no humor in the lady's eyes. Laura York wasn't kidding a bit. "Why, Laura? Why kill you?"

"Because, Mister Justice, I don't forgive either. I don't forget or forgive when it comes to blood." And then, with a wink that surprised and teased him all at once, the lady turned her horse's head away and rode back to the wagons, leaving Justice behind to wonder.

"Still smells," he muttered, and the black horse pricked its ears. He patted the big gelding's neck and rode on, watching the sky begin to darken as sundown rushed toward them.

It still smelled. Something was wrong on this wagon train, desperately wrong. There was menace in the air and it wasn't Justice alone who felt he was riding with enemies.

The lord had come a-hunting. Soon the guns would speak and the blood would begin to flow. Ruff could feel deep down that it was no good. This was a doomed expedition, but there was just nothing in the world he could do about it now. Nothing but ride lightly and keep his guns to hand, and he fully intended to do just that.

5

Dinner was at seven. The lord had summoned Justice to his table, so Justice went along; but he hadn't expected anything like what he found when he arrived.

He had seen the tent going up earlier—blue and yellow, thirty feet long, twenty wide with a removable wooden floor. Pennants flew from the tent posts. It was all very much like a circus outside, but inside was a different matter.

Ruff felt as if he had stepped into the lord's manor. A mahogany table ran nearly the length of the tent. High-backed chairs were positioned at even intervals around it. There were linen napkins and china dishes, silver and crystal, and in the center of the table a silver candelabrum. Lady Celia swept across the floor, which was carpeted with Persian rugs. She had a wineglass in one ringed hand. The other hand she held out to Justice, who kissed it gently.

"Do come in, Mister Justice. Oh, what a lovely sunset," she said, looking outside the tent briefly. "We have the dreariest sunsets at home. The air is so damp, ruinous to such displays."

The long-legged dancer who had introduced

herself to Ruff out on the plains was gone and the composed and cultured Lady Celia had returned.

"Here's Henry now," she said. Still holding Ruff's hand, she led him toward Sir Henry, who had entered by another unseen flap. The lord's eyes glowed darkly. He wore a red smoking jacket with a velvet collar, a bright-yellow scarf, and dark trousers. "Look, Henry, Mister Justice has come. Isn't that lovely?"

"Lovely," Sir Henry said. He wore a frown of disapproval on his lean face. No doubt the lord had figured it out as well—Lady Celia was just a little drunk.

She leaned against Justice, sipping white wine from her crystal glass. She wore a yellow dress that dipped low into her creamy cleavage and clung to her hips daringly. Her pale hair was precisely combed and pinned on top of her head, her makeup intact, but she seemed ready to fall apart.

"This afternoon's events have upset my wife," Sir Henry said as a grudging apology.

"Justice!"

Ruff turned to find Sir Oswald, ruddy-faced and smiling, walking toward him with an open bottle of champagne. They had a hell of a good time on these hunting trips, it seemed. "Glad you could make it, old man," Sir Oswald said. Without asking, he poured Ruff a glass of champagne. Justice placed it on the table.

"You don't drink?" Sir Henry said, nodding at the glass.

"No."

"Not on the hunt?"

"Never."

Sir Oswald chuckled a little, as if he had heard a great joke and downed his own glass.

"You don't deny yourself much," Ruff said,

glancing around the tent, which was appointed with coats of arms and draperies, although there were no windows.

Lady Celia hiccuped. Her husband glowered again.

In response to Ruff he said, "Why should I deny myself? What should I do, crawl through the thorns like a savage? I need my skinners and my chefs and my manservants. A man needs to be civilized, Justice, and if he can't have the heart of civilization in the wild, by God he can at least have a few of the trappings."

Lady Celia hiccuped again, saving Ruff from having to answer him.

Justice felt the breeze from the open tent flap and he turned as the others did. They entered then, the two dark-coated gunhands, Hawk had seen earlier, and they looked as bad as Hawk had said. They were tall and lean, the older of the two wearing a mustache that was touched with silver. He had a half-moon scar under one pale eye. The younger one's face was pocked, his lips very thin. Neither had a gun showing, but Ruff could bet they were each wearing one.

These were no two-bit thugs. Justice had seen enough punks and enough of the good ones to know professionals when he saw them.

He was seeing them now.

"Welcome," Lady Celia said, and she went to the two men, who glanced at each other and strode forward. Ruff waited as Celia led them to him and introductions were made.

"This is Ruff Justice, our scout," Lady Celia said in her best high-class accent, "and these, Mister Justice, are the Savitch brothers, Wesley, isn't it"—she asked the older man—"and Rafer."

"That's right, ma'am," Wesley Savitch said. His

voice was dry and whiskey-raw. He bowed his head slightly and stood stiffly, waiting.

"Charles!" Lady Celia called to an unobtrusive man in a claw-hammer coat who stood in a dark corner. "We will serve dinner now."

"What about Laura York?" Sir Henry asked.

"If Laura's not here, then it appears she doesn't wish to come, doesn't it?" Celia said, and her voice was much sharper. She seemed to catch herself then and smiled. "We can wait a minute or two more."

"Not necessary," Sir Oswald said, speaking from somewhere below the diaphragm. "Here's the young lady now, and charming, quite charming."

Ruff thought she was charming too. The lady reporter had shed her manly pretenses and come in a dress that matched Lady Celia's. Not in cost, perhaps, or in style, but it revealed as much if not more woman. It was a black dress, contrasting sharply with the white roundness of her breasts, which peered dramatically up over the material. Her reddish hair was curled and brushed to a sheen. There was a light dusting of freckles across her turned-up nose that Ruff hadn't noticed before.

Sir Oswald muttered a string of appreciative syllables, and Sir Henry's eyes brightened. Rafer Savitch was all eyes. The older brother, Wesley, didn't change his expression, nor did he remove his eyes from Ruff Justice.

"Well, we are all ready, after all," Celia told Charles, and the man bowed away. There was another manservant hovering in the background to hold the ladies' chairs as they sat, and then another who removed the empty wine bottles, replaced them, and disappeared silently. That was the way the meal was served—silently, efficiently. Rib roast, smoked sturgeon, quail, and crepes. And quite a lot of wine.

Sir Oswald drank his fill and then some, as did Lady Celia. Sir Henry sipped at his glass only now and then. Ruff didn't see Rafer Savitch drink anything, but his older brother drank for two, though it didn't show a bit.

"Tomorrow we break out the guns, hopefully," Sir Henry was saying. "Have you seen the weapons, Justice? No, you couldn't have. And I guarantee you'll never see anything like them again. German and Belgian gunsmiths at their best. I've a five-hundred express that will interest you. Gold and silver inlay. Damascus-steel barrels. Take down anything that walks these plains—any plains."

"But we haven't seen any game," Celia said. "None at all."

"Justice will find game for us, won't you, Justice?" Sir Henry replied.

"Yes, I'll find it for you," Ruff said quietly.

"What's the matter, Justice? Still worried about those Indians and the bandits you have out here? God, what an army these Americans have. None of that boldness one would expect."

"Maybe Mister Justice just doesn't like to hunt," Laura York said. Her eyes sparkled in the candlelight. There was a teasing smile on her lips.

Ruff shook his head. "I don't mind a hunt, meat or trophy—if there's plenty of game. I just don't like being the game."

"Maybe he don't care for blood." This was Rafer Savitch, and heads turned toward the sullen, lean gunman.

"I'm sure Justice has seen blood," Wesley Savitch put in. "Haven't you, Justice?"

"A time or two."

"Yes," Savitch said, wiping at his plate with the remains of a dinner roll. "I thought you had."

"I must say," Sir Oswald put in, "not very appetizing conversation—nor easy to follow. What are you people going on about? Anyone play cribbage here?"

Apparently no one did. Ruff Justice finished eating, and after dabbing at his mustache with his napkin, he leaned back and asked Laura York, "Are you getting your story, Miss York?"

"I will. Traveling with Sir Henry, I surely will."

"What magazine was it you worked for, dear?" Celia asked with a distinct edge to her voice.

"Not a magazine. A newspaper, Lady Celia. I'm sure you remember . . ." She glanced at the wine the lady hadn't eased up on. "*The Minneapolis Herald.*"

"Yes. I'm surprised a provincial paper such as that can afford to send a lady reporter along on this excursion."

"We have some small resources, Lady Celia."

"Do you? Good for you, dear." Lady Celia's eyes had started to glaze over. They had also started to drift toward Ruff Justice, who tried not to show as much interest as he was feeling.

"What are our chances of finding game tomorrow?" Sir Oswald asked, tipping the wine again.

"We've been tracking over buffalo sign the last few miles," Ruff told them. "Fresh. We'll maybe come up on the herd in the next few miles. Sometime tomorrow, I'd say."

"That's a rather tame hunt, isn't it?" Lady Celia asked. "Bison? It's not like elephant or lion, is it, darling?"

Her husband chose not to answer.

Ruff said, "It depends on how you do it, Lady Celia. Try it the way the Indian did in the days before the gun came onto the plains, better yet in the days before the horse. A bull buffalo can go five feet at the shoulders, and when he's mad, he's as dangerous as any horned creature walking the earth. To go in among them is something that requires some courage."

"And what about standing off a hundred yards and shooting into the herd?" she asked.

The question was provocative. She was drunk and the night bored her. Ruff had had enough of their company. Sir Oswald lit a cigar and the smoke burned Justice's eyes. He rose, saying, "Thank you for the meal. It was enjoyable. Now I think I'll turn in."

"Already?" Lady Celia asked with a slight whine. Ruff was finding her and her wine less agreeable with each passing moment. "I had party games planned."

"I rise early," Justice said. "It's been a long day."

"Sleep good, scout," Wesley Savitch said, but there was a cold glint in the man's eye.

"Can you walk me back to my wagon?" Laura York asked, rising as well.

"Of course. I'd be delighted," Ruff answered. They said good-bye to the others without much warmth. Sir Henry was sulking, no doubt the result of a few of his wife's remarks, and Sir Oswald was busy staring into his wine through a veil of blue smoke. Lady Celia might have been a little jealous or a little drunker, but her last words were snapped out.

The Savitch brothers just sat and stared, sheltering their dark secret thoughts.

It was nearly a physical relief to get outside into the night air. Bright stars winked through the long streamers of clouds, and there was a hazy glow near the eastern horizon as the moon began its ascent.

"What a party," Laura said with a laugh.

"Quite," Ruff said dryly.

She laughed again, hooking his arm with her own. "Take me home the long way. I need to stretch my legs. I didn't think you'd leave early."

"No?" They walked past a low campfire where three men sat talking, the red glow briefly illuminating their features so that Ruff could see that Sam Cukor was among them. Then they were in the shadows again, only the starlight guiding their feet. The army camp sat a quarter of a mile off, its fires burning low.

"I thought you'd want to stay with the lady," Laura York teased.

"Did you, now? What for?"

"Party games."

It was Ruff's turn to laugh. "I wasn't in the mood tonight."

"No? They say you're always in the mood," Laura said, stopping.

Ruff turned her and faced her, gripping both of her wrists. "Do they? Back in Minneapolis, you mean?"

"That's right."

"What is this?" Ruff asked. "More research for your story on Ruffin T. Justice, plainsman?"

"Maybe." The starlight was in her eyes and she tilted her chin up in a way that could mean only one thing. Since it was obviously an invitation, Ruff took her up on it, tasting her parted lips, finding them agreeable.

"Mind telling me just what is up, Laura?" Justice asked when they parted. He still held her wrists—lightly, but she wasn't going anywhere unless he let her go.

"I don't know what you mean."

"I think you do. If anyone knows, I figure it's

you. There's too much wrong with this little party. Take the Savitch brothers, for instance. What in hell is a pair like that doing along on his lordship's hunt? Don't tell me they're just hired hands—the Savitches aren't the type to hire on a job like this. Too much riding. They like to ride a chair in a saloon, and that's about it."

"Really? I don't know anything about them. They seemed like gentlemen." She couldn't quite keep the irony out of her voice.

Ruff smiled. "Sure. Gentlemen. I'd like to see the Colts they wear. I wonder if they carve notches in the grips."

"Killers?"

"Killers, and I guess you know it, being a newspaperwoman. They were brought to the lord's table tonight to be displayed. Not because Sir Henry likes their company but because he wanted to show them off, to show that he was carrying extra muscle along. Why do that? The only one there to threaten was me. What the hell have the Savitch brothers got to do with me? I've never seen either of them before, and Landis has nothing that I want—"

"Except his wife?" Laura teased.

"Leave that aside. He wouldn't hire them for that. Why, then?"

"Do you want to know?" Laura York said.

"I'm asking."

"Why, I'm quite sure he brought them here to kill you—you or someone like you."

"What are you talking about?" Ruff asked. "Why would they want to kill me?"

"They're afraid, I think. Afraid that I've brought you along to do murder for me, Ruff Justice."

6

She wasn't joking. She stood there with a straight face and told him right out, "They're afraid that you're a man I've bought to do my killing."

"You don't think that takes a little more explanation," he nudged.

"Oh, I don't think they knew who I was," Laura said. She poked impatiently at her hair. "But it seems they do. They must. That explains the attempt on my life—or yours. It explains the hired guns."

"I'm glad it's all clear to you," Ruff responded.

"I guess you can't know much about this, can you?" Laura said. She turned toward the huge rising moon and stood, arms folded beneath her breasts, watching. "To begin with I'm no newspaperwoman."

"I never thought you were."

"No? I thought it was a pretty good idea, pretending to be."

"There aren't more than three or four in the Territory—if that many—and I'd never heard of you."

"I read a story about women journalists—gave me the idea. What other reason could I conjure up for a single woman to travel along with Sir Henry and his hunting party?"

"I don't know," Ruff said. "Why did you want to anyway?"

"Because," she said, "they killed my father."

"Sir Henry?"

She was exasperated. "I don't *know* who! That's why I had to follow along."

"Come on," Justice said, taking her hand. There was a stack of boulders on a low knoll not far away, and he led her there. Laura was going to have to back up a little if Ruff was going to understand any of this, and it wouldn't hurt any to be comfortable. They sat on a flat rock that still retained the heat of the lost day, and as the coming moon grew yellow and climbed higher into the night sky, Laura told Justice how it was.

"My father was a bank teller in Climax. That's in Minnesota," Ruff nodded. He knew the small town near the Dakota Territory line. "On the morning it happened, he went to work as usual, taking a lunch bucket as he always did. Dad wouldn't eat in the restaurant in town—no, sir, not him. He was saving money. For his retirement, for me . . ." Her voice got a little misty. Ruff waited.

"Well, it was at lunchtime when they hit the bank, a bunch of masked robbers. Only Dad was there, you see. They took all the cash the bank had on hand and shot Dad as he tried to draw a gun—for what? To fight for other people's money. But then he was always that way. Duty—you know the kind of man."

Ruff guessed he did. They watched the pale moon against the long plains. Finally Laura continued.

"The marshal couldn't find a trace of the outfit. But that's Tom Jowett for you—he can hardly find his own office, he's so damn drunk all the time. He wasn't going to go chasing anyone out of the city limits, so he turned it over to the sheriff, who blamed it on the Cavanaugh gang, and everyone just gave up."

"You didn't."

"No! How could I? My father was dead. I practically lived on Tom Jowett's doorstep, but that was a waste of time. I tried the sheriff again and wrote to the United States marshal's office, but they never contacted me again."

"So you started playing lawman."

"That's right," she said sharply. "What would you have done, Justice? We don't forget blood, do we?"

"No," he answered, "we don't forgive or forget that."

"I started asking around. I never believed Jack Cavanaugh did that bank job."

"Why?"

"You know Cavanaugh. He thinks he's still fighting the Civil War. He'd have let everyone know it was him making war on the North. Besides, Cavanaugh was reported south and west a very short time later, in Aberdeen, shooting up the town. He would have needed wings. I don't think it was him."

"Logical," Ruff agreed. But what had put her on this trail? She told him in her own way.

"The arrival of Sir Henry in Climax was one of the biggest events in memory. The biggest since the town turned back Crazy Horse years ago. His party had gathered there to cross the Red River and come into Dakota. They were waiting for supplies of some sort."

"Yes?"

"The day after the robbery, they were gone," Laura said. Ruff had slipped his arm around her shoulder and she wasn't fighting it off. Now she leaned her head against his shoulder. "I found an Indian boy, an Ojibwa who told me he had seen six men ride to Sir Henry's camp. Six men carrying sacks of money."

"You told the sheriff, of course."

"Of course, but by then Jowett wasn't listening to

anything I said—my fault maybe for nagging him. Besides, he said, everyone knows how Indians lie, and did I think a wealthy man like Sir Henry would go around a foreign country robbing cigar-box banks."

"What did you tell him?"

"That I didn't know it was Sir Henry, but I was pretty sure it was someone with his outfit, pretty sure it wasn't Jack Cavanaugh." She sighed. "I had no proof. What could I do? I cozied up to old Sir Oswald and told him I was one of this new breed of female reporters out to make her reputation, and he invited me along."

"And since then?"

"Since then . . . nothing."

"Until today."

"Yes. I know what you're thinking, maybe I am on the wrong track. I haven't found any bank money or been murdered or seen Sir Henry in a robber's mask. But there was today . . ."

"You believe they thought it was you riding with me."

"Yes! Or they think I've hired you."

"Landis wouldn't think that."

Laura was getting frustrated. Her logic was a little fuzzy. Maybe she was right about all of this, but she couldn't support it with reason, and she knew it.

"I've got a couple of personal enemies on this expedition, Laura," Justice said. "I figure they were trying for me. You and Lady Celia were dressed something alike, sure, but maybe they wanted to kill her."

"Who?" she demanded.

"Her jealous husband. I don't know."

"Maybe it was just a wandering Sioux too," she said heatedly.

"Maybe so." Ruff squeezed her shoulder, but Laura pulled away.

"You think I'm foolish too. I had to tell someone. I chose you because I know *you* weren't there, in Climax. And now you're laughing at me."

"I'm not laughing, Laura," Justice said. There wasn't anything funny about their situation. There had been trouble enough in the air before; if what Laura was saying was true, they had among them a gang of bank robbers and killers. Could Sir Henry be their leader? For what reason? Maybe to support his expensive life-style. How did he support himself?

"Food for thought, isn't it?" Laura asked.

She rose and stood before Ruff, her hands on his shoulders, smiling down at him. She was quite beautiful, Ruff decided. The moonlight made her seem to glow softly.

"You could turn back to Bismarck," Justice told her. "Tell the colonel what you've told me."

"What good would that do, Justice? No, but I'm grateful that the army is here. They can hardly slaughter us with the soldiers around."

Ruff ignored most of what she'd said, and answered her question. "It would keep you alive, Laura. If these people do know who you are, then it's not safe for you to be here, and you know it."

"I'm here," she said decisively. "I'll stay." And that, it seemed, was that. She kissed Ruff lightly on the forehead and then walked off alone toward her wagon.

Justice watched her all the way, hearing the faint click of a latch after she had entered.

He rose, frowning, and stared at the moon a minute longer before walking back toward the camp and his own bedroll. There was still light in the lord's tent. Maybe Lady Celia had gotten her party games started. With the Savitches? Ruff smiled.

He picked up his bedroll and started out of the

camp again, not wanting to sleep too close to the others. Away from the camp, his senses could remain alert enough to make sneaking up on him difficult.

Ruff had his bedroll under one arm, his Spencer in his free hand, and an uneasy feeling deep in his bones as he walked to the small dark knoll south of camp. He rolled out his groundsheet and blankets and sat in the stillness watching the wagon train. It was dark now, silent. There were three or four army sentries out walking the perimeter. A light went on briefly in Laura's wagon—maybe she had pulled back a curtain—and then it went out. Ruff Justice lay back to try to get some sleep.

He tried, but the procession of hostile faces kept running through his mind: Honus Hall, Sam Cukor, Sir Henry, and the Savitches—and some, if not all of them, were on the run from the law. They were killers who would try to eliminate Laura if they knew who she really was....

The shadow detached itself from the dark of the night and the plains and collided with Ruff Justice's body. Ruff rolled aside, kicking out for his attacker's face. There was enough moonlight for Justice to see the knife in the man's hand sweep past inches from his belly, and Justice kicked again, feeling the satisfying thump as his heel cracked the man's nose.

The thug grunted and staggered backward. There was enough time for Justice to come to his feet, snatching up the big .56 Spencer repeater. The barrel was nearest to Ruff and he picked it up that way, swinging the rifle as if it were a club.

The stock of the Spencer connected with shoulder bone, and the dark figure cried out in pain, dropping the knife. Then he made his big mistake: he reached for a holstered Colt, heedless now of the noise he might make. He went for the Colt and

Justice took him down for good, to lie against the dark Dakota plains.

Ruff had reversed the Spencer, and as his attacker tried to bring up his revolver, Ruff's finger nudged the cool, curved trigger of the buffalo gun. It exploded with flame and thunder, and a .56-caliber bullet ripped its way through belly and meat and spine, jackknifing the thug, hurling him back, to lie twitching against the earth.

Justice stood over him, watching for a sign of life. He could see and hear the sudden activity in the camp as people rushed toward him. He toed the body, not recognizing the face. The man was thirty or so, whiskered, lean. Ruff glanced toward the crowd of people heading his way, crouched, and quickly searched the body.

There was nothing to identify him, no letter or bill of sale. In his coat, however, was a small paper wrapper. Just big enough to slip around a stack of dollar bills. On it was printed, "Bank of Climax."

Ruff pocketed the wrapper and stood waiting. Sgt. Wadie Cairot was the first to reach Justice. He arrived on foot, panting, his Springfield rifle in hand.

"Damn you, Justice. I knew it was you! What in hell are you up to now?"

Then he saw the dead man, and after taking an involuntary half-step backward, he went to take a closer look. "What the hell's happened here?" Cairot asked.

Other soldiers had gathered around, along with a handful of Sir Henry's men. Death attracts people, it seems. There was a good deal of shouting and guessing, and someone threw up. It was all too much for Justice. He snatched up his bedroll and started to walk away.

"Wait a minute," Cairot said, and he put his hand on Justice's arm, leaving it there until Ruff's cold stare caused the sergeant to let it drop. "Where are you going, Justice?"

"Someplace where a man can sleep," Justice said. Turning sharply, he walked away, leaving the gawkers and carrion birds to stare and chatter and speculate.

Morning would be soon enough, he thought. Morning would tell him who the man had been, and then maybe someone else would pay the price the dead thug had paid.

The dawn was bright and spectacular after a cold night. There were crimson flags and golden spikes in the eastern sky as the shifting clouds massed before the sun. They seemed to promise rain; Ruff could only hope it wasn't so. That was the last thing this dreary little party needed.

He rolled up his bed, shouldered it, and started down toward the camp, where smoke from the fires hung low over the wagons. The dew in the long grass was heavy and Justice's legs were wet before he reached the camp, found his horse, and prepared for what promised to be a long day.

He had no use for Sir Henry and his friends just then. After seeing from across the camp that Laura was all right, he walked to the soldiers' camp to share their coffee.

Billy Sondberg had seen him coming. He had a tin cup filled with hot, bitter coffee ready for the tall plainsman. " 'Mornin', Mister Justice. Heard you had some activity last night."

"Man wanted to share my blankets, is all," Ruff said.

"I don't expect you'd allow that."

"I'd have to know him a hell of a lot better," Justice said, sipping at his coffee. He asked Billy seriously. "Who do they say he was?"

"George McFarland was his name. They tell it

that he was picked up for wages in Minnesota. A drifter, a loner. No friends. No one knows a thing about him."

"That's how they tell it, is it?"

Sondberg nodded. He glanced across his shoulder. There seemed to be some activity on the other side of the camp. "Guess they want us to go to boots and saddles," Sondberg drawled. He rose, dumped out the dregs of his coffee, and said, "You take it easy now, Justice, hear?"

"I intend to, Billy, thanks." Justice checked his horse's gear and swung aboard as the trooper strode off to join ranks. Ruff watched the cavalry for a minute and started away. Hawk was riding a little dun pony when he caught up with Justice.

"Mind company?" the Arik asked.

"Not if you don't."

"All alive and everything this morning, are you, Ruffin?"

"Just about."

"Heard all the ruckus. Heard the thunder gun. Figured you was alive. Figured someone else wasn't."

"He came looking. He found it."

"Who sent him, Ruff?"

"Did I say someone did?" Ruff removed his hat and swept back his hair, waiting for Hawk to reply. It was cool this morning. Ground fog was beginning to lift from the shallow washes that cut this part of the prairie. There was plenty of fresh buffalo sign.

"I figure someone sent him," Hawk replied finally. He was looking into the distances, the lines around his eyes drawing into a tight net. "He wasn't the kind to come hunting trouble."

"You knew McFarland?"

"Knew him?" The Arik lifted one shoulder in a shrug. "Worked with him—what little work he did.

He was a bottle hound. Liked to get drunk and sit looking at his pistol, hoping for a chance to shoot it."

"Doesn't sound like much."

"He wasn't. Not enough to come after you. Not on his own."

Ruff nodded. He had never thought that McFarland had come on his own. He hadn't come looking for something to steal; he had come to kill, and Justice had never so much as laid eyes on him before.

"Why did he want you, Ruffin?" Hawk asked, his eyes returning sharply to Justice's face. Ruff fished into his shirt pocket and handed the Arik the paper band he had found twisted up on the thug's body. Hawk looked at it, pushed out his lower lip thoughtfully, and handed it back. He might have said something, but just then a long, dark, living thing had appeared among the low hills to the south.

It was a buffalo herd, and a good-sized one, up with the sun and now slowly grazing its way south.

"It'll make the lord happy," Hawk said.

"Sure." Ruff scowled, his eyes lifting to the horizon. "Think anyone's told him, Hawk?"

"Told him what, Ruffin T.?"

"That where you find buffalo you find Indians?"

Hawk just shook his head. No one had told the lord, and if anyone had, he would have laughed off the danger. He was confident in their numbers, in his guns. But then Sir Henry Landis had never seen Indian fighting. Ruff and Hawk had, and they weren't laughing.

Stone Eyes would be out there and he would want their treasures. Sir Henry's wagons, his finery and tents, his horses and guns, he would want the women.

He would want their blood.

7

Leaving Hawk to prepare for his skinning chores, Ruff Justice told Sir Henry what they had found. The lord's eyes were a little red and puffy this morning. He rode a long-legged sorrel horse that was tricked out in fancy tack. The lord himself wore a dark coat, cream-colored trousers, and a flat, wide-brimmed white hat.

"How many at a guess?" he asked Ruff, his eyes sharpening at the promise of a hunt.

"Plenty enough for you to find meat and a trophy head, I promise you."

"Yes, but how many?"

"Seven, eight hundred," Ruff answered, "maybe more."

"Fine. Let's have a look at them, shall we?" At a wave from the Englishman a small man with pouched eyes and a hound-dog expression rode forward. "See to the guns, Cox. We'll hunt this morning."

"Yes, m'lord," the little man said.

He rode off toward the lord's wagon, passing Lady Celia, who was riding toward them with excitement in her eyes. Ruff couldn't tell what had gotten her so excited, but she let him think it was him. She reined up sharply and eyed him with that frank look she used to her advantage. Then she smiled brightly, "Good morning, gentlemen. Are we hunting this morning?"

"We are," Henry said almost expansively. He had come to life at the mention of the buffalo, and Ruff wondered about the kind of man who needs to kill to live. "Justice has found the herd for us."

"How clever of Justice," Celia said. Her eyes were clear and wide, her face unblemished, her yellow hair brushed loosely across her shoulders. There wasn't a sign of the night's drinking on her. Nor was there any sign of the long-legged commoner Lord Henry had taken back to his manor. Lady Celia had regained her composure, yesterday's shooting incident forgotten, or at least put aside.

"Do you shoot?" Ruff asked the lady as they rode side by side, angling southward. They watched Lord Henry lean forward across the withers of his sorrel, eagerly awaiting the first sign of the herd.

"Not well. Henry's been trying to teach me but he's impatient and I'm a poor student. This is my first hunt, you know. I used to wait at home for the crusader's return. And he would return—at intervals."

"What made you come this time?" Ruff asked.

Her bright eyes flashed as she turned her head toward him and offered him a sparkling smile. "Curiosity, Mister Justice. Simple curiosity as to what could cause a healthy man to prefer the slaughter of wild animals to bedding his wife."

There wasn't much to say to that, so Ruff let it drop; the herd had begun to appear now anyway, here and there like pools of shadow among the golden-stubbled knolls. A groan seemed to come up from the massive herd as they approached, but it was only thunder from the cloudy eastern skies.

Sir Henry rode to the crest of a knoll and waited

for them to go by. His hands clenched his reins tightly. His lips parted, revealing even teeth in what was less a smile than some sort of emotional rictus.

Ruff watched the lord and then glanced at the lady. Her white blouse revealed the outline of her full, ripe breasts, and the wind drifted through her long, silky yellow hair.

Maybe, he thought, there *is* something wrong with the lord.

The herd was comparatively small. In the old days—only a few years ago actually—the same number would have flowed past that spot, a dark, living thing that had to keep moving to survive.

There were plenty there for Sir Henry, and he sat mesmerized until Sir Oswald arrived, along with the gun-bearer and the skinners. On their heels were the Savitches and still farther back a cavalry contingent—Cairot would want to take some meat for his boys too.

Cairot was a good soldier who had only one shortcoming, but that one bordered on the maniacal—his hatred of Ruff Justice. And his hatred was tied up with his idea of what his lost brother would have wanted.

Justice couldn't waste a lot of time thinking about Wadie Cairot just then. The lord had gotten down from his horse and was preparing his guns while the others watched. Sir Oswald, looking dark-eyed and dumpy, went about it with almost equal enthusiasm. The lady looked bored.

Wesley and Rafer Savitch weren't watching the lord; they were watching Ruff. Both wore dark suits that were somewhat stained, and dark hats. Ruff saw the amusement in their eyes but he couldn't figure what they thought was so damned funny.

When Laura York arrived, she was angry.

"Where have you been?"

"Doing my job," Justice answered mildly. Her cheeks were highly colored and it surprised him.

"Why in the world didn't you come by this morning? I just found out what happened last night. I heard the shot, of course, but someone said a prowling wolf had been killed. Ruffin"—her eyes searched his—"they tried to kill you, didn't they?"

"Someone did." Then he handed her the currency wrapper and she stood looking at it, fingering it like a holy relic.

"It's from Dad's bank."

"That's right."

"Then that man was with them! Do you realize this is the first tangible evidence I've found. Now we can—"

"Now we can what? We've proven that McFarland was one of that gang, but McFarland's dead."

"We can talk to Sergeant Cairot. If you tell him what's happened, what you've found, then perhaps he can invoke martial law or something, search the wagons, because the money has to be here somewhere, doesn't it?"

Laura had started to speak in a rapid fire that built as her excitement did. Ruff smiled at her eagerness but he had to burst her balloon.

"Cairot wouldn't walk across the street to spit on my grave, Laura. I couldn't ask him anything."

"Then I could."

"And if you were to find out nothing? If they don't know now that you're trying to track the killers they sure will after you've spoken up. Besides, Cairot isn't going to listen to you either."

"But"—she held up the wrapper forlornly—"we have this."

"Yes, and so do hundreds of other people. Every businessman in Climax, for instance."

"But a man like McFarland shouldn't have had it, and we know the bank robbers are here."

"We know. But we can't prove it. Cairot's no lawman and no NCO in the world is going to take the risk of offending a man as important to his superiors as Lord Henry Landis."

"But that's the whole problem, don't you see?" Laura gripped his arm. "No one suspects him, no one has the courage to investigate him. Not the marshal, not the sheriff. No one. That's how he gets away with it."

"Easy. You could be right, but you could very easily be wrong. Why does it have to be Sir Henry? He seems to have all he wants. Why not the Savitches, using him? Sam Cukor? Honus Hall, or some of the Englishmen?"

"Or the lady," Laura said perceptively, but too sharply. "Maybe she needs money to get away from her lord and master."

"Maybe," Ruff said cautiously, "just maybe."

"Justice!" Sir Oswald called. "Are we ready?"

"Just a minute." Ruff spoke more softly to Laura now. "Be patient. I think you're onto something, but hurling a lot of accusations around isn't going to help. You settle down a little and things will go better."

She started to argue, but Justice stilled her protest with a kiss; it was quick and hard and unnoticed by everyone—except for Lady Celia.

"So," the blonde murmured as Justice passed her. "It is the common woman you prefer, after all."

There was an odd expression lurking in her eyes, turning up the corners of her mouth. Justice couldn't quite figure it out. The lady, it seemed, was not amused. But what had Ruff ever promised her? Maybe she needed a man around badly, something

67

she hadn't had for years with Sir Henry away. Or maybe there was something not quite right in the lady's head somewhere . . .

"Justice!" Sir Oswald had taken a little telescope out. He was studying the herd intently. Beside him, a shooting brace had been thrust into the ground. This was a long wood and brass pole with a loop for Sir Oswald's rifle at its top. The gun-bearer stood by with the rifle, an inlaid gun of German make with a bore you could put your thumb in.

"Look at that one, Justice. Massive. What do you think? Take him?"

The glass was given to Ruff, who was guided until he found the bull buffalo that had Oswald so excited. The man was right, it was a good one, its massive shaggy head supported by a thick neck, and a heavy, muscular body. The head, Ruff supposed, would look good on a man's wall if you were the sort who liked to have a stuffed buffalo staring at you for years to come.

"He's good," Ruff said. "You'd look a long time before you could find a bigger one."

Sir Oswald made a small satisfied noise with his tongue and gestured for his rifle. It was settled into its loop and the nobleman got behind the sights. Sir Henry meanwhile had picked out his own bison, and as Oswald sighted on his bull, Henry's rifle spoke. As the smoke drifted before Ruff's eyes, he saw a big black buffalo go down to its knees before rolling onto its side, dead.

At the sound of Sir Henry's shot, Sir Oswald too touched off. He missed his shot in his excitement and his bullet tagged a smaller cow behind the bull. The buffalo, unexcited by the lead hornets humming past, contined to graze contentedly.

Sir Henry had a second target and he fired now, bringing it down. Sir Oswald tried again, scoring on his bull this time, which went down bawling, and reloaded.

Sir Henry fired a third shot and scored again. It wasn't hard to hit something. Now Wesley Savitch, Winchester in hand, got into the act. He shouldered the .44-40 rifle and began levering through the cartridges, switching his sights with each shot, taking three buffalo quickly down.

"Landis," Ruff said, "you've got your trophies, you've got your meat, leave them alone."

Sir Henry didn't bother to glance at Justice. It was his hunt and he didn't need a scout telling him what to do. He fired again, the big rifle thundering, sending a deadly bullet across the plains. Yet another buffalo went down.

"There's another," Sir Oswald said happily. "Near the rear of the herd."

Savitch had emptied his rifle, and now he and his brother stood firing their revolvers into the herd. The noise on the knoll was overpowering, the smoke dark and acrid, but below the buffalo still grazed, moving around the dead and dying ones without concern.

A dozen were down now, two dozen. Still Sir Henry continued to fire.

"That's enough, Landis," Ruff Justice said angrily. He touched the lord's arm and Sir Henry turned on him.

"Damn you, Justice. Mind your own business. Find the game and then step back."

"This isn't a hunt, it's a slaughter."

Sir Henry shook him off and got back to his shooting. Behind Ruff the Savitch brothers continued to shoot. Sir Oswald was finding a new and more desirable trophy head every few minutes and killing yet another bull.

There wasn't much to do but shoot the hunters

or walk away. Ruff turned and walked away, past Laura and the smiling Lady Celia, the smirking Wesley Savitch, and Honus Hall, who had unlimbered his own rifle to take down half a dozen buffalo.

The guide deliberately looked at Justice before lifting his weapon again to kill yet another bull. Justice kicked him on the knee. Honus Hall went down with a howl to writhe on the grass. Justice picked up the red-bearded man's rifle and emptied it.

"With them maybe it's just ignorance," Ruff said. "You been around long enough to know better, Honus." Then he threw the rifle back into Hall's face and walked on, away from the shooting, the smoke, the needless death.

He found Hawk on the far side of the knoll. The Arikara Indian was squatting against the earth, holding the reins to his paint pony. He stared into the vast distances at nothing in particular.

Justice stood beside Hawk. The sting of gunpowder was still in his nostrils. The guns seemed to go on forever.

"Kill 'em all," Hawk muttered once.

Justice didn't say anything. There wasn't much to say. It was a simple slaughter, a taking of many living things, an ending of life for no purpose except that the killers liked to see death, liked to have that power.

Stone Eyes wasn't going to like it either.

The Sioux had been a reservation Indian, but he had gotten into a squabble with the post trader, killed him, and fled to the wild, taking quite a few followers with him. More had come to his totem, as Stone Eyes had success in skirmish after skirmish. He had promised to drive the white man out, to bring back the buffalo.

Something like this wouldn't set well with the renegade. And he would know about it.

The guns roared on.

Someone in Stone Eyes' camp was bound to stumble over the wasted dead littering the earth, buffalo killed, not for their meat or their hides but simply for the sake of killing. Stone Eyes just might take that as an act of war.

When the guns finally fell silent, Hawk rose, picked up his small bundle containing his skinning knives and sharpening stone, and headed off toward the site of the slaughter. Justice retrieved his own horse, swung aboard, and rode slowly off. He didn't figure anyone would miss him just then.

On the plains the wind was cool and cleansing. Ruff brought the black into a canter, watching the long grass bend in the wind, watching the clouds mass and darken the sky, trying not to think about human beings and their ways.

He knew the area where he now rode. Grand Coulee was to the north, angling through the knolls and scattered cottonwoods and oaks. To the south and east the broken hills began to rise, and on their flanks cedar trees clung tenaciously. That was hard country, the canyons twisted and raw, red earth showing like open wounds. There was water there, but there always seemed to be too little or too much: small stagnant ponds that could poison man or horse, or roaring white water that could sweep them away.

It was grizzly country and cougar country. As little as Justice felt like doing it, he supposed he would have to find the lord his trophies—and probably the sooner, the better.

Now antelope bounded away as Justice rode nearer to the uplands. How many of them would the lord want? A hundred? Justice gritted his teeth and continued on.

From time to time the skies spat a few cold drops of rain. The wind increased and the few trees Justice passed waved frantic arms at him. The land began to rise around him and eventually he was surrounded by broken bluffs and hills that rose abruptly and then fell away without any pattern. There were scattered pines in the washes where shallow creeks rambled across rocky beds. Justice saw mule deer twice, and once the tracks of a big cougar.

He gave the cougar little thought. What bothered him now were the tracks he had been riding over for the last quarter of an hour. The tracks of horses, many horses. They had passed this way very recently, and that could only mean trouble. No one who wasn't trouble was riding the plains just now. Whoever it was feared no one, and that meant two things.

They had plenty of guns and they were ready to use them.

8

The skies were darker yet, the wind a cold muttering in the canyons as Ruff rode farther into the reddish badlands. Rain had begun to drizzle down steadily, making things still more miserable.

The tracks Ruff had been following crossed the stream and picked up a trail on the opposite side. Ruff counted eight horses, all shod. That meant whites, and that meant trouble.

The only white man crazy enough to be out here just now was Jack Cavanaugh. Cavanaugh with his private army and his hatred of everything "Yankee." To Cavanaugh the war hadn't ended; it had only been discontinued while the South gathered its strength. He hated blue uniforms, Connecticut accents, and the Stars and Stripes. He was a very dangerous man.

Cavanaugh was big and dark and scowling, and he had a kind of personal magnetism that drew men to him—the angry, the discontented, the half-mad. Cavanaugh raided small settlements, robbed banks and stage coaches, and burned out any suspected Yankee sympathizers. He left death behind him wherever he went.

Ruff unsheathed his Spencer and rode warily. The rain continued to fall, screening him, glossing the rocks and the trunks of the cedars. Intermittent thunder rumbled down the slopes.

What was Cavanaugh doing up here?

Ruff had to admit it was the only place for miles around where a large body of men could hole up with some sense of security, far enough from Fort Lincoln and the army, yet near enough to a source of supplies. Still, the Sioux were roaming the area and it didn't seem all that smart.

Ruff saw the man ahead of him before he saw Justice. Ruff pulled the black from the road and went up into the trees. He swung down and crouched, waiting, the Spencer in his hands, the rain falling softly through the pine and cedar forest.

He hadn't seen much of the man, just a flash of red color. He was lucky he'd been able to see that much—he happened to glance up a moment before the horseman, whoever he was, rounded a bend in the trail and disappeared into the trees again.

Ruff waited motionlessly. It was cold and his limbs grew stiff. The sky was almost completely dark when he heard the soft progress of hooves against damp earth.

Suddenly the man was there. He had stopped to put a dark rain slicker on over his shirt, but a bit of red still showed above the collar. He was dark and hawk-nosed and a stranger to Ruff. He rode the trail as if he hadn't a care in the world, nothing to fear at all.

Justice let him go by and then started upward into the hills. This time he didn't use the trail but wound through the trees. If it was Cavanaugh, he would have lookouts posted.

The water was beginning to form rivulets winding its way downslope. Ruff passed a long mossy boulder that was sheeted in a thin waterfall. The thunder became constant and the rain fell harder. Justice began to wonder if he hadn't got a little too nosy this time; he didn't want to be out here at night, but it looked like he was going to be.

He rode uphill until the darkness and rain closed around him, making travel impossible. Wet and cold, he turned his horse down the hill again.

"I know he's up there," Ruff muttered. Cavanaugh had to be close by, but no one was going to find him on this night.

Justice reached the canyon bottom and started back toward the lord's wagon train. The rain was still falling, and the creek beside the trail had become a roaring, frothing menace, shuttling down the canyon with the speed and sound of an express train.

The shot was close, very close. Ruff saw the stab of crimson flame, the dragon tongue flicking from the muzzle of a rifle, and he flinched reflexively. It missed him, but the rifle bullet tagged Justice's horse. The black reared up in pain and panic, throwing Justice from the saddle. He hit the ground hard and lay there stunned. Then the ambusher made the most serious mistake he was ever going to make—he must have thought he'd hit Ruff because he came out of the willow brush with his rifle held across his body. His dark slicker was glossy in the rain and the bit of red shirt showed clearly at his collar. Ruff had made his own mistake—the man had seen him earlier and he had taken a chance by waiting for the scout to come back down the trail.

The bearded man came forward, intending to check the body, and if necessary to put a round through Ruff's head to finish the job.

Ruff didn't intend to let him.

He rolled to one side and came to his knees, drawing the big blue Colt on his hip, bringing it up to fire twice into the body of the bearded sniper. The man's mouth opened in astonishment, sudden fear, and anguish as Ruff's bullets ripped into his body, kicking him back, to lie sprawled in the mud.

Ruff rose to his feet, his hair in his eyes, and walked to where the sniper lay—this man who had come to spill the blood from his body and leave him lying in the cold darkness.

"How does it feel?" Justice asked softly, but the man didn't answer.

Ruff holstered his Colt and crouched over the body, searching it. The sniper didn't have much with him, only a pocket knife, a hundred dollars in gold money, and a folded wanted poster, which would have matched his face well without the beard. Ruff straightened up, reloading and holstering his Colt. He looked upward into the hills.

"Dammit, Cavanaugh, I know you're there."

There wasn't much he could do about it, however—not right then. Maybe if morning was clear, Cairot could take his detachment up into the hills to look for the rebel. At the least a rider could be sent back to Lincoln to advise the colonel that Cavanaugh's hideout had been found.

For now there was nothing to do. Nothing but get out of the driving, cold rain and back to the wagon train.

Ruff found the black and looked it over carefully, finding the groove the sniper's bullet had cut across its neck. The black was mad as hell and in some pain, but sound enough. Justice swung aboard and headed back.

When he found the wagons, the rain was coming down even harder, the wind twisting it into strange patterns and images. Ruff found Sgt. Wadie Cairot huddled inside his small waterproof tent.

He hadn't been asleep, but his eyes were pouched

and angry by the light of the tiny fire at the tent's flap. He looked up at Justice as if he would have liked to kill him then and there. Wadie hadn't forgotten.

"What the hell is it, scout?"

"I think we're riding right into Jack Cavanaugh's hideout."

"You do, do you?" Cairot said, his mouth twisting into a sneer. The wind touched his miniature fire and it leapt toward the NCO like a crimson and gold tongue. "What makes you think that, Justice? Last we heard for sure Cavanaugh was down on the Heart River."

"I ran into a man up in the hills."

"Cavanaugh?"

"No." Justice squatted down. He didn't like this man, not at all, but it was important to check his temper and get through to Wadie Cairot's little brain.

"Someone told you Cavanaugh was up there?" Cairot asked slyly. Now Ruff could smell the whiskey on the man's breath.

"No, he didn't tell me anything. He's dead now—tried to ambush me. His name was Wally Heinz." Ruff gave the sergeant the folded wanted poster. "He was carrying this on him."

Cairot looked at it for a long while. Then he shrugged. "So?"

"So, no lone man is going to be holed up in these hills with Stone Eyes around."

"Wally Heinz was." Cairot threw the poster into the fire, where it darkened and curled.

"I'd like you to send someone back to Lincoln and tell Colonel MacEnroe what's going on."

"And what is going on, Justice?" Cairot asked, peering up with those pouched eyes. "You saw a man and you shot him."

"He has to be one of Cavanaugh's men."

"The hell he does."

"Will you take a patrol up there with me tomorrow to look for Cavanaugh's camp?" Ruff asked, trying a new tack.

"No. Why should I? No one sent me out here to look for Cavanaugh's camp. They sent me to watch this wagon train, and if I pull off to go on some wild-goose chase, then that's just what I'm *not* doing. Leaving them unprotected isn't what I was ordered to do, not on the word of no bullshit scout."

"Cairot, you're not protecting them much if you ride right into Cavanaugh's camp, are you?"

"Cavanaugh wouldn't attack no cavalry patrol."

"Cavanaugh hates blue uniforms. He'd try it if he took a notion."

"I'm tired of this, Justice. Cavanaugh's down on the Heart River. It ain't my job to chase him down. I'm doing my job."

"You won't send a man back to Lincoln."

"No, damn you, go yourself if you want to, if you're so damn sure Cavanaugh is out there." Wadie Cairot's face had turned nearly purple. His hand clenched and unclenched near his holstered Schofield pistol. He wasn't going to listen to anything Ruff Justice had to say, not even if it meant running into a private army and risking his charges to the likes of Cavanaugh.

Ruff rose and ducked out of the tent without another word. The rain was dying down but the wind was bitter cold. There was still a light in Sir Henry's wagon, and Justice headed that way across the dark camp, passing a lone soldier who barely looked up. It was a miserable night to walk guard duty.

Ruff rapped on the door and it was opened by a small bald-headed man in a dark suit. Sir Henry stood behind him with a wineglass in his hand, looking curiously toward the door.

"Yes?" the valet asked.

"I have something important to tell Sir Henry."

"His lordship . . ."

"Justice? Is that you?" Lady Celia called. She appeared in a silk dressing gown with her yellow hair down around her shoulders, her green eyes bright. "It is! Come in."

Justice stepped inside. The valet looked at him cross-eyed, took a minute to close the door, and then disappeared into a small compartment. Ruff glanced around the oversized wagon, noticing the incredibly lavish furnishings. There was a red velvet chair and settee, silk curtains, a Turkish rug on the floor, and a silver lantern on each wall. Sir Henry traveled in luxury when he roughed it. But it didn't keep him in any better temper than Cairot. He snapped at Justice, "What prompts you to intrude like this, Justice?"

His eyes went to the floor. Justice was dripping water all over a Turkish rug that depicted a sultan on a tiger hunt. Justice supposed the rug cost a lot; he didn't care just then.

"We're running into trouble. If we keep heading the way we're going, we're going to find ourselves in something we can't handle."

"The Indians?" Lady Celia asked, fingering the pearl necklace she wore with her dressing gown.

"No, the outlaw Jack Cavanaugh. I'm almost sure his camp is ahead, not far from here."

"You have evidence?" Sir Henry asked, sipping at his wine before placing the glass down on a teak table that, like everything else in the wagon, was fastened to the floor with brass fittings.

"No, but I've got the man's scent. Believe me, he's there."

"You've told Sergeant Cairot?" Sir Henry asked, turning away to light a small cigar.

Ruff couldn't see his eyes as he spoke. There was something nasty in his tone however. "I've told him."

"And?" the lord demanded. His back was still to Justice.

"And, nothing. Cairot and I have a personal grudge that tends to overshadow his logic. You see—"

"I know all about your 'personal grudge,'" Sir Henry said, turning back, "and it's about what I would expect of you."

"It is, is it? That's odd, considering you don't know me. You don't know me at all, Landis."

"I know you well enough, dammit! You were given to me to help guide me to where the game is, to help us find water, and I suppose to keep an eye out for the Indians. The responsibility for making decisions doesn't rest on your shoulders, however. I make the decisions. Sergeant Cairot provides the additional security. That is our arrangement, and if you don't like it, I suggest you return to Fort Lincoln. We'll make do with the personnel we have left."

"I'd consider it—if you would let Lady Celia and Miss York go with me."

Sir Henry laughed. "You think I'd let a scoundrel like you take my wife and leave?"

"If you want her to stay alive."

"What do you say to that, dear?" Sir Henry asked.

Lady Celia smiled. "I'm afraid the idea is preposterous, Mister Justice. I've come on this hunting trip to be with my husband, not to turn and run off."

"And I don't think Laura York would go either. Do you?" Sir Henry demanded.

Justice didn't answer. No, Laura York wouldn't

go. She was sticking with this party until she found out who had killed her father while robbing that Climax bank.

Which left Justice in an impossible situation. He couldn't get the ladies out of there, couldn't talk Sir Henry or Cairot into turning back. Yes, he could turn and ride out himself, but that wasn't his way of doing things. The army had sent him along and MacEnroe was counting on him to try to keep the lord and his lady out of trouble.

Besides, he couldn't leave Laura alone. Someone was onto her, it seemed. Someone wanted her dead.

"Now, if you'll be so good, Justice, my wife and I were just having our nightcap. We'd like a little privacy. Tomorrow you'll find me something to hunt, won't you? A great bear, perhaps. At least I hope so. Certainly something more challenging than the buffalo you found."

That wouldn't take much, Ruff thought. It had been a great challenge indeed to stand there on the hill and slaughter the buffalo. It took about as much skill and courage as stepping on a stinkbug.

The man stood with his head tilted back, looking at Ruff with disdain through half-closed eyes. The cigar burned between his fingers. He smiled and said, "Good evening," and Justice went out into the storm, his anger starting to build again.

"Damn them all," he muttered to the cold and blustery night. "Damn them. They won't quit until they're all dead."

And that was just what was going to happen. They were going to roll on into the hills until Cavanaugh or maybe Stone Eyes found them and descended upon the undermanned wagon train. Sir Henry thought his forty men were plenty. He was wrong. He was dead wrong.

9

The morning was bright and clear, a few high clouds floating across the deep-blue sky. The earth was damp and wet, and the horses breathed steam as they were led to be harnessed or saddled. Ruff saw Hawk and lifted a hand. The Arikara waved back but not very cheerily. He knew.

"Hi!" Ruff turned at the sound of Laura York's voice. She sounded cheerful, although what right she had to feel that way he didn't know.

She also looked beautiful on this windy morning: her reddish hair tucked under a tan hat, her matching tan suit neat and close-fitting. She rode her horse up beside Ruff and he leaned against the animal's shoulder, one hand gripping the pommel of her saddle.

"You're gloomy this morning," Laura said.

"I've got a few reasons."

"Not me, I hope." She laughed.

"No, not you."

She looked around her at the activity of the rising camp. "We're going on, then."

"Yes. Did you hear something?" Justice asked.

"Celia was saying something about Jack Cavanaugh being out here."

"He is."

"I guess you're the only one who thinks so?" It was a question and Ruff answered it.

"I seem to be, yes, but they'll find out."

"You could be wrong, couldn't you?"

"Sure," Ruff answered. "I could be wrong." But he didn't think so. "Did you have breakfast?" he asked.

"Tea and eggs with the lord and his lady. I interviewed them through the meal."

"Still trying to make them think you're a newspaperwoman."

"Trying, yes."

Ruff looked around. "Let's ride on out, all right?"

"If you don't mind," Laura said with some surprise. "I didn't think it was safe out there."

"As safe as it is here. I'd rather have you with me than leave you with Honus Hall and those Savitch brothers."

"Now that you mention their names," Laura said as they walked toward his black horse, "I haven't seen much of them lately—especially Hall."

"Maybe he's supposed to be out hunting up game, but I've never cut his tracks. Something funny's going on here, Laura."

"Oh, I know that," she answered.

Ruff had swung aboard his black horse and now the two of them rode out onto the long grass plains, looking ahead toward the shadowed hills. "I can't figure out which one of them might have done it," she said.

"Killed your father?"

"Yes. It's Sir Henry's wagon train, of course, and you tend to think he must be responsible for what's going on around him, but I can't imagine an English lord riding around playing highwayman in America."

"Maybe Sir Oswald," Ruff said jokingly.

83

"You never know, do you?" Laura was quite serious. "I've found out something about the relationship between those two brothers. Did you know that Oswald has virtually nothing—no lands or estates or money? All of the family fortune was left to the oldest son—that's Henry Landis."

"So Oswald just has to sort of tag along and play the fool."

"It seems so. That would be enough to destroy a man after a while, wouldn't it?"

"I don't know," Ruff answered. "It would depend on the sort of man he was, I suppose. I can't see Oswald trying to kill his brother."

"Why not? Of course he'd have to kill Celia too."

"He would, would he?" Ruff's eyebrow lifted.

"Sure. And someone did, or so you seem to think—*try* to kill her, that is."

"What's that got to do with a bank robbery in Minnesota?"

"Oh, Ruff, I wish to God I knew. Sometimes I wish I'd forgotten the whole business. I can't solve this thing. I've been hoping to get a glimpse of some of the stolen money, but no one has shown any of it."

"No reason to, out here," Ruff said. He guided them up a broad valley. The hills rising around it were reddish and bright, with new grass in patches. There were low, wind-twisted cedar trees and higher up some spruce dotting the land. They rode south, angling away from Cavanaugh's camp. Ruff hadn't forgotten Cavanaugh and was keeping his eyes open for tracks.

"Yesterday . . ." Laura hesitated and then went on. "I searched some of the wagons while you were away, while they were killing buffalo."

"That's dangerous, Laura, very dangerous."

"I know it is, but dammit all, Ruff, I'm getting desperate."

"Be patient, just be patient. I've a feeling that this thing will open wide soon. Everyone is too edgy. Someone is bound to talk out of turn. Look." He pointed at the ground.

Laura saw nothing. "I don't know what you mean."

"Cougar tracks. A big boy. Look at your horse. He's still around here, close by. The tracks were made after the rain."

"So what will you do? Find it for Landis?" Laura asked, and there was distaste in her tone.

"I suppose so. Let him get his trophies and get the hell out of here as soon as possible. Get the whole wagon train of you out of here."

"When you talk like that . . . you really *are* worried, aren't you, Ruff?"

Instead of answering, he reined up. When Laura halted her horse, he leaned across and put his arm around her waist. Drawing her to him, he kissed her, kissed her until she barely had the breath to gasp.

"Maybe we should get down for a while."

"That was what I had in mind," Justice said. They were higher up along the reddish slopes now. Where they had halted, a small grove of oaks sheltered them from the wind. Below them, the canyon funneled away to the green flats. The wagon train was only a distant collection of tiny toys rolling ever so slowly toward them.

Ruff took Laura's hand and walked with her to the oaks. When she removed her hat and shook her head, her reddish-gold hair tumbled free. The sunlight fell through the dark tangled branches of the oaks. He kissed Laura again and she returned his kiss, pressing her breasts against his chest. Her hand slowly opened and her hat fell to the grass.

"You're supposed to be scouting," she said quietly. Laura's fingers toyed with the fringes of his buckskin shirt. He could feel her weight against him, the press of her thigh and pelvis, of her breasts. Her blouse was open at the throat beneath her tan jacket, and her cleavage, pale and smooth, drew his eyes and then his lips. He kissed her there and felt the drumming of her heart.

"Let 'im find his own big cats," Ruff said. He turned and led her still farther into the trees, to a green hollow between three giant boulders where the sun shone warmly.

He held her neck with one hand and kissed her again as his free hand held her buttocks, drawing her to him. She shivered a little and stepped back.

"Warm," she managed to murmur, and then she slipped out of her jacket. Ruff's eyes lighted with pleasure. He studied the way her breasts strained against her white blouse. She wore nothing beneath it, her nipples standing taut.

"There," Laura said. She dropped her jacket.

"Still kind of warm, isn't it?" Ruff asked. He drew her to him again and his fingers began to undo the buttons of her blouse, releasing those firm, uptilted breasts from the restraining fabric. His lips followed his fingers down, and Laura rested her hands on his head, letting a small sigh escape her lips.

"Is that better?" he asked.

"Nearly." Laura opened her blouse and shrugged out of it, to stand there, beautiful and compelling, her pink-budded breasts receiving Justice's approving inspection.

Then she turned her back, and as Justice stepped to her and kissed her shoulders, the nape of her sun-warmed neck, her round pink ear, she unfastened her belt and let her skirt slip to the ground. She wore some kind of fancy underthing, and after a moment's embarrassment as Ruff turned her and looked deeply into her eyes, she stepped daintily from that, too, and then lay back on the grass and gazed up at him.

"Now you," she said, and it was more or less an order. It was about the only kind of order Justice didn't mind taking. He winked, pulled his shirt over his head, and then tugged off his boots. Placing those and his gun belt aside, he unfastened his trousers.

Laura gasped a little, half-smiled, and then reached out for him as Justice, naked and ready, stood before her in the mottled shade.

"Now, aren't you something?" she said.

"Something you like, I hope."

"Let me find out," Laura said, and Justice got down to his knees before her. Her hands ran up his thighs and wrapped themselves around his thick shaft. She gazed down at it in wonder, her fingers working back and forth, around the head of it, and then suddenly she lay back, rolling onto her hands and knees.

"Please," she said, and Justice did his best to please her.

He eased up behind her as she reached back and groped for his erection, positioning him and then slowly sinking onto it as she bowed her head and lay quivering against the earth.

Justice eased it home and the woman's head came up. She gasped as if she were having trouble catching her breath, and then reached for his sack, cupping it, holding him close to her as if afraid he would move away.

Justice hadn't given that possibility a thought. He

kissed her smooth buttocks and straightened again, arching his back, thrusting in as deeply as possible. He felt a deep demanding pulse in his loins as Laura began to sway against him, to rock and softly moan, her body becoming soft and damp as Justice worked against her, his hands now on her thighs. He held her tightly to him as he felt his sudden hard climax coming over him.

"Justice . . ." She gave a little quiver and then a small stifled shriek as she finished, going forward on her face, her body shaking as Justice reached his completion. She lay there, touching him where he had entered her, biting on her knuckle. Her skin was flushed hot, her heartbeat racing. Justice reached around and cupped her breast, kneading the nipple, and her hand went over his and held it there.

A Sioux warrior came out of the trees with a whoop and the rustle of leaves, and Justice rolled to one side, grabbing for his Colt. The Colt was always at hand, where he knew he could grab it if necessary.

It was damned necessary now. The warrior whooped exultantly, figuring he had scored a great coup. He had a long-haired man's scalp and a white woman. He had found them laughing together beneath the trees. It would be easy, or so he thought. All he had to do was bury his hatchet in the white man's head. Then he could slowly take the woman, teasing her, playing with her, seeing if she could laugh with a Sioux.

It should have been so easy.

But the war cry had risen from his lips, his feet had made too much noise against the leaves, and the white man was warned.

Still the Sioux could not fail to win. The man's gun was put aside and he would not know where it was immediately, and even if he did, there wouldn't be time to draw it, to fire before the warrior could cleave the long-haired white's skull.

That was the way his reasoning went as he leapt at the white scout, even as he saw the man roll to one side, away from the body of the white woman, who screamed.

The impossible happened then. The white man had known exactly where his Colt was, and he had leapt for it without hesitation. When the Sioux warrior began to strike downward with the steel-headed ax in his hand, the Colt in Ruff Justice's hand exploded with thunder and flame and the red-hot lead bullet plowed through flesh and entrails, shattering bone.

The .44-40 bullet went up through the Indian's ribs and touched his heart, and it was over as the great muscle was opened up by searing lead.

The Sioux was flung backward and he sat down, his war ax in his lap, the blood pumping from his mouth. There was a small blue hole in his chest. He looked at Justice, nodded, spoke a word Ruff didn't understand, and then toppled over, dead.

Justice sat on the grass a moment longer, his legs trembling slightly. Then he rose and walked naked to the body. He could hear Laura York sobbing, but that was a peripheral sound. He was listening for other things, looking for other signs of movement in the trees and on the hillside.

"Get dressed," he told her.

"Are there others?" She was hoarse and frightened.

"Let's not wait to find out. Get dressed!" He said it more sharply that time, and Laura did as he said, hurriedly dressing as Justice stepped into his own trousers and pulled his shirt over his head.

He still saw nothing moving. He took the time

then to go to the woman and calm her. He smiled and held her to him, kissing her cheek lightly.

"I'm scared," Laura admitted. There was a single tear coursing across her cheek. "Do you always live like this?"

"Not when I can help it. Get your hat, all right?"

"We're leaving?"

"Just as fast as we can. That was one of Stone Eyes' warriors."

"How could you know that?"

"His belt. It was army issue. He killed a soldier to get it, Laura."

She glanced to where the Sioux lay, and looked for just a moment as if she might be sick. But she pulled herself together and picked up her hat, tucked her hair up and under, and tugged the drawstring tight beneath her chin.

"You think there are more, don't you?"

"I think there are more."

They walked to where the horses stood. Ruff had his unsheathed .56 Spencer out and ready, riding in the crook of his arm. He held the reins to Laura's horse as she mounted, his eyes searching the slopes, the canyon. He hadn't seen any Indian tracks down below, but then he hadn't seen this one's sign either.

"Maybe he was alone—a hunter or messenger," Laura suggested hopefully as Justice swung aboard the big black and turned it north toward the flats.

"Maybe," Justice said grimly. He rode with his head swiveling in all directions, his eyes sweeping the slopes. There could have been a thousand Sioux hidden in those hills.

"Why not?" she asked in exasperation and fear.

"And what if he was? Someone will still miss the man. When he fails to return from a hunt, when he doesn't come through with the message he was carrying, when he misses his dinner. He'll have a friend, a brother, a father, who will miss him."

"And then . . ."

"And then they'll come looking for him, maybe a small party at first. They'll find us, and if we haven't cut and run, they'll see that we never get the chance to run anywhere at all."

"You're frightening me."

"Good. I'll tell you a few stories guaranteed to frighten anyone, all about Sioux hospitality. I'll tell you a few war stories, and then maybe when the time comes to make a decision, you'll have the sense enough to realize we've got to turn back."

"No," Laura said. She seemed to puff up, her spine stiffening. "I'm not turning back, Justice. So long as the wagons roll on, I'm man-hunting. You ought to understand that."

He just looked at her. He understood that, all right, but he didn't figure he understood Laura York at all.

"It's not worth dying for, Laura."

"It is to me, Justice. To me, nothing's worth more than finding the man who killed my father and seeing that he's punished. Not even my own life."

Then she clammed up and wouldn't say a word, kneeing her pony into a faster run. Muttering imprecations against womankind, Justice rode with her toward the wagon train below.

10

Sir Henry listened intently to Justice's report, glancing occasionally at the somewhat disheveled Laura York. Celia Landis listened, too. Cairot was there, looking puffy and half-drunk, along with the smug gunhawk Wesley Savitch, who leaned against the wheel of the lord's wagon.

When Justice was finished, Sir Henry asked, "How big was the cougar, would you say? Record size?"

"Lord Landis, I'm telling you that I tangled with a Sioux warrior out there."

"*One* Indian." Sir Henry sniffed.

"And there'll be more."

"Now you can see the future, can you, Justice?"

"I can tell which way the wind's blowing," Justice answered tightly.

"What's up?" Honus Hall had arrived. The scout wore a dirty pair of black jeans with the knee out, and a dirty red shirt.

"Justice has found a cougar for me, a large one," Sir Henry said. It seemed he had understood nothing of what Ruff Justice had told him.

"Goin' after him?" Hall asked. His little eyes were dull as he turned his head and spat.

"That is why I am here. If Mister Justice refuses

to help my wife and myself with this cat, will you go?"

"That's why *I'm* here," Honus Hall said. "You're paying."

"Your wife!" Justice said.

"Of course," Sir Henry replied calmy. "I have promised Celia a shot at the big cat. She's most eager."

Ruff turned to stare at Lady Celia Landis. "You're going to do this, Lady Celia?"

"I might as well learn something about hunting, Justice. There's no sense in coming along to remain behind in the wagon."

"The Sioux—"

"No one else seems worried about one Indian," she said with indifference. Her eyes were glowing oddly again and Ruff decided that she was drunk already, though it was early. The woman was on a road to self-destruction—maybe she couldn't handle being the commoner wife of the great lord.

"Listen, Lady Celia," Justice said. "Maybe it's right for you to learn to shoot, to hunt with your husband, but you don't want to practice on a mountain lion, believe me."

"Oh, well," she said with a little wave of the hand. "I'll have a gun and so will my husband . . . and we'll have you with us, won't we?" She smiled again, invitingly this time, and then with a little wave of the hand walked away, her blond ringlets bouncing.

Sir Henry gestured to Hall and his gun-bearer, and they left the wagon too.

"Something, ain't it, Justice?"

Ruff turned to look into the eyes of the lounging Wesley Savitch, the dangerous, cautious Wesley Savitch. He had his thumbs hooked into his low-riding gun belt.

"Did you say something, Savitch?"

"Don't get excited, Justice. I reckon you're looking for someone to hit right now—it's not me. I was just making a general comment on things. You'd think they were all crazy, wouldn't you? This Hall now, I thought he knew something about rough country. You'd think he'd know better than to go out there right now. What do you suppose they're up to, Justice?"

"I don't know, Savitch. Maybe you know."

"Not me." Wesley Savitch laughed dryly, breaking off into a cough. "I'm just along for the ride."

"Why are you here?" Justice asked, pressing it. "Who invited you in?" He stepped nearer to Savitch and stood looking down at the pale-eyed gunfighter.

"Me," Savitch said with a smile, "I invite myself. I'll be seeing you, Justice. Take my advice, watch your back." Then he tugged down his hat and sauntered off, leaving Ruff and Laura York alone.

She came to stand beside him and his arm automatically went around her waist, supporting her. "What are you going to do?" she asked finally, looking up into his eyes. The wind lifted her red hair slightly across her worried blue eyes.

"Go hunting cougar, I guess. What else is there to do?"

And while he was out there, he was going to be watching his back. He was definitely going to do that. Laura, on the other hand, was going nowhere. She had had enough, and even if she didn't think so, Ruff did. She didn't fight him when he kissed her and told her to stay put. The wagons would be at rest and she could use the opportunity to crawl up into her wagon and lie down.

"Make sure you lock your door too. Stay inside. None of this searching the other wagons."

She agreed meekly, brushed his cheek with her lips, and walked off toward her wagon. Ruff watched her for a while and then rode over to the army camp.

Soldiers milled about aimlessly or squatted down, rifles in hand. Billy Sondberg lifted a hand but said nothing. Ruff nodded to Reb Saunders and then swung down from his black when he found Wadie Cairot standing alone, glowering at the plains. Cairot smelled like whiskey again.

"What do you want, Justice?" the NCO growled.

"Just came by to see if I could get you to change your mind about turning us around."

"I heard about the Sioux."

"Did you now? Well, you should know that where there's one, there's more. No one ever said you were a bad NCO, Wadie. You've got sense enough to know we're riding into bad trouble here. We ought to turn back."

"Maybe." Cairot was subdued momentarily. "But it ain't my job. My job's to protect the lord best I can while he hunts. There's danger here, sure, but Colonel MacEnroe knew that when he sent us out. What am I supposed to do? Overrule my commanding officer? Not on your life."

"The colonel didn't *know* Cavanaugh was out here. He didn't *know* Stone Eyes was in this area. We do, Wadie." Justice waited a long time for the answer. Cairot was struggling. He wanted to live too, and as Justice had said, the sergeant was no fool when it came to knowing about the Indians.

"No," he said at last. "Colonel's orders."

"Wadie . . ."

"No, dammit, that's it, Justice!"

"Send a rider, then, take a message to Lincoln."

"And what the hell good is that going to do? What would the message say, 'Colonel, we're out here and Ruff Justice is seeing boogie men, can we come back?' "

"You could—" Ruff began.

Wadie Cairot turned his back and walked away. Everyone seemed to be doing that to Justice this morning. After a minute he decided to give it up. He borrowed a canteen from Reb Saunders, rinsed off a little, and rejoined the hunting party.

They had a buffalo calf taken alive earlier to be used as bait, and they all looked up at Justice, who nodded agreement. That would bring the cat down. Assuming you really wanted to call 250 pounds of muscle, claw, and fang to come toward you.

Celia held a silver-mounted double rifle in her tiny hands and Justice asked her, "You sure you want to go along on this hunt? It's going to be dangerous."

"You really like that little redheaded woman, don't you?"

"I'm talking about the hunt, Celia."

"*Lady* Celia," she said, her eyelids lowering a little. "I'm sure we'll be safe enough. We've got plenty of guns along."

Ruff glanced at the lord and lady, at Honus Hall. "Maybe too many guns," he said. Then he checked over his own weapons, borrowing a rod to clean the Spencer, which had burned powder that morning.

And likely would again.

They rode out in a loose line, Lady Celia and her husband, Oswald, Honus Hall, Ruff Justice, and Hawk, who would have to skin out the cat if they got it.

"No soldiers," Hawk said.

"No, but there should be. Landis doesn't think we'd have much of a chance at finding the cat if we fill the hills with men."

"He's right."

"He's right," Ruff agreed. "But I'd rather have the soldiers than the cougar's hide."

"A cougar blanket is good magic, Justice," the Arikara Indian said. "Wear the cougar hide and it gives a man courage."

"So I've heard. I'm not sure Landis needs more courage, though. He's got enough courage—or foolishness—to last a man a long while. I still can't figure him."

"I know him," Hawk said. "The hunt, Justice. I have seen others who live for it. The stalking, the sudden fight. Then, when the animal is dead, the excitement is suddenly over. It is time to hunt again."

"I guess you're right. I've about given up trying to figure out this crowd." He added, "Hawk, you know there will be Sioux."

"I know this."

"Watch for signs. If we find anything at all, we're pulling out if I have to drag them out of the hills."

"I will watch. Justice, where is the body of the Sioux you killed?"

"Why do you want to know that, Hawk?"

"I want to go to it and abuse it. Take its hair."

Ruff nodded. The hate of the Arikara for the Sioux was very deep. He told him where the body could be found.

Justice took the lead as they entered the long canyon. Honus Hall was not far behind. Justice didn't like having him at his back, but he figured it was safe enough as long as Hawk was back there too.

They wound up the trail Justice and Laura York had taken earlier. Thinking back to that brought a smile to Ruff's lips. That was quite a woman, Laura York. He only hoped she was staying out of trouble back at the wagon camp.

Justice held up the black. He lifted his hand and Sir Henry came forward eagerly. Ruff was pointing at the ground.

"Those are his tracks?"

Justice nodded. He glanced up at a feeder canyon to their right. It angled up sharply, twisting through cedar and spruce trees, past jutting red bluffs. This was rough country, cougar country. He swung down and looked more closely at the tracks.

"How long since he passed?" Sir Henry wanted to know. Sir Oswald had also swung down and he stood there, pink and round and unassuming, his eyes on the tracks.

"In the last few hours," Ruff told them. "The grass hasn't sprung back up yet." He stood, dusting his hands. "He'll be up there somewhere."

"Shall we have a look?" Sir Henry asked.

Ruff nodded. He waited a moment longer, studying the rugged canyon. Not only was it a place for cougar but an ideal ambush spot for the Sioux if they were around.

He swung aboard the black horse and started up the slope through sage and sumac until they broke onto a trail of sorts again. There was only a little water running along the bottom of the canyon. The trees began to hang over the trail, ancient, stunted cedar.

When the canyon dead-ended abruptly, it surprised even Justice. He held up his horse and looked upslope. Only a cat or a man could climb there. The horses weren't going any farther.

"It will have to be here, then," Sir Henry said. "We'll stake the calf here."

Sir Oswald looked suddenly jittery. There's a certain uneasiness that goes along with knowing you're in the bush with a wild animal strong enough to kill.

The buffalo calf had been on the haunches of

Hawk's horse, a sack tied over its head to keep it from bawling. Now Hawk untied it and slipped the sack from its head. It immediately began bleating, a pathetic sound, one that was certain to draw the cougar if it was still in the area.

Ruff drove the stake with a rock and Hawk strung the calf to it. Then they rubbed stake, calf, and thong with buffalo fat. They wanted to cover any man scent that might drive the big cat away.

"Where do we wait?" Sir Oswald asked nervously. His brother stood coolly surveying the hillsides. Lady Celia yawned.

"In the rocks downwind." Ruff pointed. "That's best. You'll have a good shot at him."

Sir Oswald looked dubiously toward the red bluffs where the broken cedars grew. He didn't like the idea but he said nothing.

Lady Celia spoke up. "I'm certainly not climbing up there! I doubt I can, anyway, in my skirt. I'll leave it up to you men."

"You can't stay here alone," Sir Henry said.

"Justice will stay," Celia said. "He'll watch me."

"For God's sake, Celia . . ." The lord's mouth tightened, but he gave in out of frustration. "All right, have it your way. Hall, Oswald and I are climbing into the rocks."

"We'll be in the trees, there," Ruff said.

Sir Henry grunted something, shouldered his rifle on its woven leather sling, and began climbing. After a minute Sir Oswald followed, moving tentatively up the face of the bluff.

"I go now," Hawk told Justice. He looked at Celia, his black eyes revealing nothing. "I will come back when I hear shots."

"Can you find it?"

"I will find it, I remember what you said," Hawk

99

answered. Then he was gone, silently moving down the canyon.

The lady asked, "Where's our skinner going?"

"To savage an enemy's body," Ruff answered.

"To what? How primitive the man is. It's disgusting."

"Not to Hawk. It's important to him to discredit the dead warrior. Don't talk about him as if he were nothing either. He was, is a great warrior whose time has gone."

"Like you?" Lady Celia asked sharply.

"Maybe so," Ruff Justice answered thoughtfully. The calf bawled again, interrupting his thoughts. "Let's get up into the trees."

"Will I have a chance at it?" she asked eagerly. Her eyes had brightened suddenly, the way her husband's sometimes did when he spoke of killing.

"Maybe. But probably not. Only if your husband and Sir Oswald both miss. That's not likely, is it?"

"No," she said. She seemed distracted. "No, it isn't."

They were in the trees now. Coolness fell over them, and the scent of spruce trees was rich in their nostrils. Justice found a little hollow that overlooked the bait. Above them was a bluff of decomposing red sandstone where nothing grew. It was still. A butterfly danced past Justice's eyes. From time to time they could hear the buffalo calf.

"Why don't you go back, Justice?" Lady Celia said. "You hate this, you don't like any of us but that lady reporter."

"I'll go back. If you come with me."

"Gallant, aren't you?" Her hand fell on his arm.

Ruff glanced at it. "It would go on my record if I lost a titled lady out here."

"Just a dancer."

They were sitting on the ground now. Pine needles and sparse grass brightened the raw umber of the earth with green.

"Dancer or a lady," Ruff Justice said, "what's the difference?"

"There's a lot of difference, Justice." She removed her hat and placed it to one side. The sun was in her golden hair. Her eyes looked tired. "Maybe you wouldn't understand."

"Try me."

"For one thing"—she leaned near to him—"a dancer could kiss you like this." Her lips were hot and searching as they found his briefly and then were pulled away.

"And a lady?" Justice asked.

"It takes a lot to shake you, doesn't it?" she asked, looking at him with wonder.

"I've been shaken."

"If you . . ." She hesitated and shook her head. "I like you, Justice. I wish you'd just turn around and ride home."

"I told you before—"

But the cougar interrupted his sentence, the cougar and the thunder of the guns.

11

"There he is," Celia said, getting to her feet. There was a gun in Lady Celia's hands, a double .460 express that had taken down a rhino and a Bengal tiger in its time. She stood and swung the muzzle up before Ruff had located the mountain lion.

Now he did. It was behind them on the bluff, and he saw the tawny flesh of the animal leaping toward Lady Celia, saw just for a moment the red of its mouth, the white fangs, the pale color on its belly. Lady Celia was smiling.

She was smiling until she squeezed the trigger, and nothing happened.

The hammer of the engraved .460 fell on an empty chamber and the click was so loud that Justice could hear it above the snarling roar of the cougar.

He didn't have time to think. He must have drawn the Colt even before the lady stood, even before she had aimed the hunting rifle at the attacking mountain lion.

The Colt spat flame and death, bucking four times against Ruff's hand as he fired into the muscular golden body of the big snarling cat.

Lady Celia screamed as the cougar slammed into her body and they went down in a bloody, tangled heap. Ruff watched for any signs of movement from the big cat, but there were none. It was dead, its body pressed against Lady Celia, who was sobbing still.

"Please," she said. A bloody hand stretched out to Justice. "Help me."

Ruff rolled the cougar away from her and helped her to her feet. She was stained with the animal's gore, ripe with its scent. She stood against Justice, her chest heaving, her eyes streaming tears, and he held her, stroking her hair.

"Kiss me," she said frantically. She looked at him with sad deep-green eyes and said, "Please kiss me. I'm only a dancer."

Justice kissed her, long and hard, holding her until the trembling was gone.

"Now this is very lovely."

They stepped apart as Sir Henry, his pants torn, rifle in his hands, came through the trees toward them.

"Your lower instincts rise again, I see," Sir Henry said to his wife, and then without warning, he backhanded her, slapping her face so that her mouth dripped blood and she staggered back.

She fell, but Landis never saw it. Ruff Justice didn't give him the chance. A right hand shot from the long-haired scout, whistled through the air, and tagged the lord beneath the ear. He sat down hard, and Justice hovered over him, panting. Then he bent over and picked up Sir Henry's weapon, winging it into the trees.

Sir Oswald was coming on the run, panting, struggling, but Justice ignored him.

Sir Henry shouted, "I'll have you—"

"What? Drawn and quartered?" Justice demanded. "You won't have anything done to me, Landis, nothing that scares me enough to let you beat up your wife. Maybe where you come from you can hit people and no one will say anything to you, stand up to you, but you're here now, in my country."

"Damn you, Justice," the nobleman said, "damn you!"

"Sure. Look around, you see what happened here? She was scared. Look at her dress. The cougar hit her. She was just holding on to me for support. Maybe I'd be doing the same thing if I had a big cat hit me." Ruff was looking now at Sir Oswald. "Crack that rifle open, Oswald. The lady's!"

The Englishman did as he was told. Celia had gotten up again, but Sir Henry, glowering, still sat on the ground.

"She tried to shoot the cat with that."

Sir Oswald looked up, bewildered. "But . . . it's empty."

"That's right. Empty." Justice shook his head. "Someone gave the lady an empty gun."

"But why?" Sir Oswald asked. "Surely it was just an oversight."

"Was it?"

"You're not suggesting someone wanted harm to come to Lady Celia? Besides, no one could know the lion would attack her."

"No, no one could know."

Hawk burst from the trees and Ruff tensed, thinking that the Sioux had returned. But the Arik ran to where Justice stood and whispered to him.

"Honus Hall is dead. His neck is broken."

"Where?"

Sir Oswald interrupted, "What is it now?"

Hawk told Ruff, "I'll show you."

"What's the matter?" Lady Celia demanded, and Ruff told her.

"Dead? But how?"

"Let's find out." Ruff looked to Sir Henry. "Are you coming?"

Sir Henry struggled to his feet. He walked along behind Hawk. Justice followed Henry Landis, Celia on his arm. They found Honus Hall's body at the foot of the cliffs.

"He must have fallen," Sir Henry said. "When I heard Justice's gunshots, I scrambled down as quickly as possible. Oswald, did you see it?"

"I? I saw nothing. I followed you down. Hall remained behind. He must have lost his footing, that's all."

And it was difficult to disbelieve the little pink man. Difficult, but not impossible. Ruff had never liked Honus Hall, but he liked being this close to a murderer even less.

"Cut the calf free," he told Hawk. "I'll bury Honus."

Ruff had just started to drag the body of Honus Hall nearer the bluff so that he could cave rocks and earth in over it when the shots reached his ears.

Distant, like the popping of firecrackers. They meant someone was fighting and probably dying.

"What is it?" Sir Henry asked.

"The wagons," Justice said. He was already going toward his horse, Hawk behind him.

"Sioux?" Hawk asked, but Ruff could only shake his head.

"Now," he told Sir Henry as the nobleman swung up on his horse as well, "now we'll see if you had enough guns to do the job."

But Sir Henry was pale with fear. His quarry didn't shoot back. Blood still trickled from his ear and his jaw was swollen where Ruff had hit him. Celia, smeared with drying gore, looked somehow more sure of herself now than the lord did.

"What are we doing?" Sir Oswald wanted to know. His lip trembled as he spoke.

"What!" Justice spat, "We're going down there.

There's a fight going on and our people are involved."

"Our people! A bunch of American soldiers and our servants."

"That's right. Them and a woman," Justice snarled.

"I'm not going," Sir Oswald said. He started to back away. "I'm not a soldier. I'm not going down there."

"Don't be a fool, Oswald," Celia snapped. "What are you going to do out here—alone?"

"I don't know, but I'll be alive. I'm not going down there."

Justice's guard was down, his thoughts on his companions and on the battle below, out on the plains where Laura York was. It wouldn't have done him a bit of good to react sooner, but still he was chagrined when the six armed men stepped casually from the woods, rifles leveled, and their leader said to Sir Oswald, "Ah, come on. Let's all go on down there. It should be just about over by now anyway."

"Who in God's name are you?" Sir Henry demanded. The man with the gun turned his head and spat. "It looks like I'm the man in charge, don't it?" He squeezed off and his Winchester belched fire, a bullet whipping past Sir Henry's head, tearing a chunk of bark from the cedar tree behind him.

He was a tall man, dark, with a scar running across his forehead. He wore black except for a red scarf.

"You Cavanaugh's men?" Ruff Justice asked.

"You guessed it, scout. You the one that killed Wally?" the outlaw demanded.

"Who?" Ruff's face was deliberately blank.

"Yeah. Get his weapons, Frank," the leader said

to another man. "Go over him good. A man like that's liable to be carrying something tricky. Al, take a look at these fancy dudes' gear, see if they've got anything. You—Indian—put down rifle, understand me?"

Hawk understood. His face wooden, his eyes hard, he dropped his rifle. His hands were quickly tied behind his back, as were those of all the men.

They went over Justice well enough, lifting his Spencer, unhitching his gun belt, and tossing it aside. They also found the little skinning knife inside his boot. One of the outlaws pocketed it.

"Now," the leader of the badmen said, "let's get on down and see what the damage is."

"I'll see you hung," Sir Oswald said, and the outlaw rapped his skull with his rifle butt. Sir Oswald went down to hands and knees, head hanging, blood trickling from a deep scalp cut.

"You'll see who hung, Chubby?" The outlaw laughed. "Pick him up, boys, throw him across a horse." When they had done that, the outlaw took Sir Oswald by the hair and lifted his head. "You'll never see Avery Donne hanged, chubby. You'll be lucky if you see tomorrow. Lucky if Jack Cavanaugh don't put you on a spit and roast your fat little body."

Then, roaring with laughter, the outlaw let go of Sir Oswald's head. He turned, taking the reins of the horse that had been brought to him, and swung aboard, Justice's eyes on him all the while.

He had heard of Avery Donne, heard too much about him. He was one of Cavanaugh's earliest recruits after the war. Donne himself had spent the war years in Kansas and Missouri as a civilian raider. His gang had made Quantrill's outfit look like schoolboys. With a man named George Hewitt, Donne had raided, burned, and raped his way across bloody Kansas, across strife-torn Missouri. Their relationship had lasted as long as Donne had use for Hewitt. One night over a card game Donne had murdered the other outlaw.

They started down the long canyon with Avery Donne as their guardian angel. The men with him looked hard; aside from that, they didn't seem to have much in common. One of them had a prematurely gray beard and looked very intelligent, like a misplaced college professor. There was a white-haired kid who looked like the idiot of all time. That one wore three revolvers: two in silver-mounted hip holsters, one around his neck on a string.

The trouble was, stupid as he looked, Ruff would have bet he could use those guns in his sleep—maybe all three at once. Cavanaugh had no use for people who wouldn't kill or didn't know how.

Sir Henry seemed to be bearing up fairly well, though the lord was white, shrunken. At least he was sitting up straight in the saddle. Sir Oswald only moaned from time to time.

Lady Celia had her head up. There was blood on her, and her face was smeared with dirt, but she looked confident.

Ruff didn't feel confident. Not a bit. The shooting had stopped on the plains beyond the mouth of the canyon. That meant the fighting was over. Donne was leading his outlaw patrol down toward the wagons—that could only mean that Cavanaugh had won. In another minute Ruff would have a chance to begin to see things for himself.

They emerged from the canyon as the clouds from the north drifted in, staining the plains with dark shadow. It was getting late already, late and cold.

The wagons stood on the prairie as if deserted. You had to look closely to see their protectors—

sprawled on the ground or hidden behind them. There were horses, mostly cavalry horses, wandering riderless across the grasslands. And now, adjacent to the wagons Ruff saw the enemy. A bunch of horses stood shoulder to shoulder while men held their reins and others searched the wagons.

Cavanaugh must have had fifty men there. Many of them wore dark rain slickers, expecting the storm to hit. All of them wore plenty of firepower.

There wasn't much doubt as to who had won.

Silver and silks, glass and furnishings were being hurled from two of the wagons. Sir Henry cursed under his breath and Lady Celia's nostrils flared, her eyes opening wider.

"That's not necessary. What's that all about?"

"I couldn't say, lady. You'd have to ask Cavanaugh."

"And that," Celia Landis said, "is exactly what I intend to do."

She didn't have to wait very long. Two men came riding out from the wagon train to greet Donne and his prisoners. The man in the lead wore a Confederate uniform with the insignia of a brigadier general. He rode a white horse and carried a tasseled saber.

Justice had never seen Jack Cavanaugh before, but he knew he was looking at him now. When he reined up before them, Ruff could see the cleanly chiseled features of a man in his early forties. His hair was dark, his sideburns long, his mouth and lips a little too full, slightly degenerate. There was something very unwholesome in his eyes, eyes that switched from point to point, focusing and darting away.

"Celia," Jack Cavanaugh said. Somehow it didn't surprise Justice. Sir Henry was a different story.

His eyes popped out of his head, and what had been a chalk-white face turned beet-red.

"You are addressing my *wife*! You know my wife!"

Cavanaugh continued to look at her. "You're as lovely as ever. As you can see, I am still fighting for the cause."

"I thought we'd never be together again," Celia said, and there actually seemed to be real emotion in her eyes. Apparently she really cared for Crazy Jack Cavanaugh.

"What in bloody hell is all of this?" Sir Henry shouted. Donne prodded him with the muzzle of his rifle, but Sir Henry didn't seem to feel it. "How could you know my wife? What can she have to do with a bunch of bloody renegades like you?"

Cavanaugh's eyes merely flickered to Donne, and Donne yanked the Englishman from his horse. Sir Henry landed sprawling on the ground.

"Get up," Donne said. "Get the fat one down too. Lock them up in the first wagon."

"There is one thing, Jack," Celia said, touching the sleeve of the bloodiest man on the plains gently. "Those men are destroying the wagons. Hardly necessary, is it?"

"Old habits," Cavanaugh said with a laugh. "They hoped to find the money, I suppose."

"Oh, the money. Do you want that now?"

"No, there's time later," Cavanaugh said. It was all as polite as a Sunday lemonade party down South. Cavanaugh's eyes danced a little crazily, but the rest of it was quiet, restrained.

Donne interrupted, "What about the scout and the Indian?"

"I don't think we need them. Kill them," Cavanaugh said as an afterthought.

"That wouldn't be honorable, Jack." Celia

touched her bloody dress. "Ruff Justice here just saved my life. He and his friend," she added as Ruff and Hawk exchanged a glance.

"All right, then. Tell me all about it later. Put these two with the soldiers, Avery."

"The lady reporter," Ruff said. "How is she?"

"Reporter?" Cavanaugh's eyebrows lifted and fell. "The woman is a newspaper reporter?"

"That's right," Celia said.

"What luck! She'll be useful. Don't harm the woman, Donne. Put these two friends of Celia's in with her. For now."

"For now" could have meant anything. Justice had an idea what it might mean. He didn't want to disappoint Celia by killing them in front of her, but Jack Cavanaugh didn't have much use for the long-haired scout and an Arikara Indian.

They were taken from their horses and led to the second wagon. Sir Henry and his brother were already locked in the other. Now Donne opened this one and Justice was pushed inside to land on the floor. Before he could rise, Hawk was pushed in as well and the door slammed shut.

"God, Justice"—the voice was Laura York's—"what are we going to do now?"

And Justice couldn't answer her. He didn't have the faintest idea in the world what anyone could do now with the army patrol beaten and Jack Cavanaugh in total control. He scraped himself up off the floor and went to Laura, who sat, hands folded together on Sir Henry's bed, which had been ripped apart in the search for money.

Ruff sat next to her and took her in his arms, holding her close. Someone shouted an order and the wagon lurched forward and they were driven deeper yet into the devil's lair.

12

They rolled on for mile after mile into the broken hills where Jack Cavanaugh had his hideout. The trail was winding, steep, and narrow. More than once the wagon Ruff Justice rode in was tilted up sharply and had to be pulled back by many hands—or ropes. They couldn't see outside; they could only hear the voices through the air vents Sir Henry had installed in these specially designed coaches.

None of what they heard was informative; most of it was profane.

Ruff spent the time trying to mentally map their course, hoping to come up with something the army could use—if he ever managed to get back to Lincoln, which didn't seem very likely right then.

"What are they going to do with us?" Laura York asked. It wasn't the first time she had asked. Ruff hadn't found a good answer for her yet.

"It'll be all right."

"They won't let us out of these hills alive."

"Maybe," he said, offering her a pat and a smile. "Cavanaugh said he had use for a newswoman."

Laura said bitterly, "I can imagine what kind of use he might have for me."

"I don't think he's that kind. Somehow I don't get

that feeling... Watch out!" They had hit a nasty bump and the wagon lifted and then pitched sideways. A heavy-framed picture fell from the wall and narrowly missed Laura's head.

"What kind of man is he, then? Mad?" she asked.

"Probably."

"What is it he wants? Publicity?"

"That's my guess."

Laura was pensive. She looked at Ruff soberly and said, "He'll find out I'm not a reporter, that I haven't got a newspaper to give him publicity."

"That's the one thing he mustn't find out," Ruff said with urgency in his voice. "You're our best hope of getting out of here, Laura. He'll treat us right if only to impress the outside world. Don't admit that you're only posing as a newswoman, no matter what."

"Someone *knows*, Ruff."

"No. Someone suspects, that's all. Even if they happen to find out that your father was a bank teller, that he was killed, you stick to your story. Convince him that you're what he hopes you are."

"Top of hill," Hawk said. The wagons had leveled. The horses seemed to be pulling easier now. In another few minutes they were on a downgrade. "Pretty soon now, I think," Hawk said.

He was right. In another half-hour, with darkness beginning to fall, the wagons were halted and they were let out to stand blinking at the hidden valley where Jack Cavanaugh's camp lay.

Ruff saw Sir Henry, badly shaken, led out of his wagon. Sir Oswald still lay inside. Not far away, the surviving soldiers stood together, some of them manacled. Billy Sondberg was there, alive, as was Wadie Cairot, the sleeve of his uniform shirt nearly torn off.

The mountains rose sharp and gray against a

deep-purple sky. The flanks of the mountains seemed barren, but in the valley itself tall pines grew in deep ranks.

"All right, scout, you come along. Lady," Avery Donne beckoned, "you with him."

Hawk started forward as well but Donne motioned him back with his rifle.

"I don't suppose Jack has much use for an Indian. You stay, chief. Al! Take the chief here with the soldiers and them Englishmen. Put 'em all in the old bunkhouse."

"Why don't we kill 'em now?" Al asked. He was a pleasant-looking man with a patch, a whiskered face, and a split nose.

"I don't know why. Jack don't want 'em killed now."

Ruff whispered to Laura, "Not while the newswoman is here to see it."

The four soldiers were herded past. Behind them came Sir Henry's servants, gun-bearers and camp laborers—six men altogether. Ruff didn't see Sam Cukor. It was no great loss to the world if he was gone.

He did see the Savitch brothers—they weren't tied up or bruised or bloodied. They still wore their guns and stood among Cavanaugh's men, laughing, gesturing. Wesley Savitch seemed to feel Ruff's gaze on him and he turned slowly, smiled, and winked.

"Now we know who hired them on, don't we?" Ruff said.

Donne said, "Shut up. March along over there. The cabin with the lantern in the window. Move it, Justice, and don't get cute. Maybe Cavanaugh wants you alive, but me, I don't care."

Dusk had turned the sky above the pines to deep purple and orange. Long crimson streamers wound among the building clouds. Somehow Justice wasn't able to enjoy the sunset much.

They reached the small cabin and Donne opened the door. Justice was shoved in, Laura York held back. She gave a little gasp as Donne gripped her arm tightly.

"Hurt? Don't worry," he said, laughing. "I won't bother you, girlie. Not while Jack wants you. 'Course, when he don't want you anymore, that's another story. There aren't a lot of women out here."

The door remained open as Donne spoke. They were deliberately taunting Justice. He tried not to let his anger show. Sir Henry and Sir Oswald arrived a minute later and were put into the same cabin as Justice. The door was closed; the last thing Ruff saw was Laura York looking helplessly over her shoulder at him.

As a matter of course Ruff made a tour of the cabin; the place had apparently been used as a lockup before. There were no windows and the ceiling and walls were sound.

"God," Sir Henry said. Ruff glanced that way. The Englishman had sagged onto one of the four makeshift cots—leather straps nailed to wooden frames and covered with ticking and straw.

The lord didn't look so arrogant now, or so proud. To Justice he looked like a middle-aged man who has suddenly realized that life can kick back.

It had just kicked him in the teeth.

"Is he all right?" Ruff asked, nodding to Sir Oswald, who lay sprawled facedown on another cot.

"I think so. I don't know." Sir Henry made a gesture of futility. "What's going to happen now?"

"Only Cavanaugh knows. And maybe your wife."

"Celia! How could she have done this? Why?"

Ruff said, "You'd have to ask her." If he didn't know, Justice wasn't going to tell him. By the light of a low-burning lantern on the wall Justice examined Sir Oswald's wound. The skull was split, there was a nasty purple knot half the size of a man's fist there, but it didn't seem to be dangerous. Unless something had gotten damaged inside.

"Are you all right?" Ruff asked the Englishman.

"Think so," Sir Oswald said without his lips seeming to move.

"Can you sit up?"

"Don't know, old boy. Try."

Ruff gave him a hand and eventually Sir Oswald managed to get into a nearly upright position. He leaned against the bunkhouse wall, his chest rising and falling too rapidly, a trickle of blood worming its way down his cheek.

"Just take it easy," Ruff counseled.

"Only way I can, Justice," Sir Oswald answered. A faint smile brushed his lips.

"What is going to happen now?" Sir Henry repeated. He looked lost, haunted, suddenly worse off than his brother.

They got part of the answer to his question a few minutes later. The door to the cabin slammed open and a stocky man with a cow's face entered carrying two buckets of water and a stack of towels over his shoulder. Behind him Al stood watching with his single eye.

"You," the outlaw said to Sir Oswald, "get up and wash up. All of you. You're dining with Cavanaugh."

Sir Oswald shook his head wearily. "I don't think I can . . ."

Al crossed the room and savagely kicked the rickety bed under Sir Oswald. The two front legs collapsed and the Englishman spilled onto the floor. Ruff felt his fists bunch, his jaw clench, but he held himself back. It wouldn't help to start anything now, and Al had that rifle in his hands.

Maybe he wouldn't have it later on. Justice was developing a positive dislike for the one-eyed gunman. He crossed the room, eyeing Al, and carefully helped Sir Oswald to his feet. Al laughed and went out, taking his flunky with him.

"What do we do?" Sir Oswald asked blankly.

"You heard the man. Wash up. Dinner at eight." Justice kept his tone light, but he wasn't very cheerful inside. They were in a desperate position and he knew it. Prisoners of a madman with a private army that boasted somewhere between fifty and a hundred men, cut off from the rest of the world in this mountain hideout, miles from Fort Lincoln or any other possible help. They were completely at Cavanaugh's mercy, and he was not known to be a merciful man.

Ruff stripped off his buckskin shirt and washed up as best he could, wiping back his long hair with his fingers. Sir Oswald followed suit, cleaning his bloody face and his hands, which were stained and dirty from falling down.

Sir Henry sat staring at the wall.

"Come on, Sir Henry," Ruff said, "let's get washed up."

"Why is she doing this," Sir Henry said to the wall. "Why would she?"

The wall didn't answer. Ruff nudged Sir Henry toward the cold bucket of water and handed him a towel.

When Al came back, he was smoking a cigar. It wasn't a very good cigar but Al probably didn't know it. He still had his rifle and that smug look on his face. Behind him stood Wesley and Rafer Savitch.

"Let's go," Al said.

Ruff led the way out, stepping into the cool night air under the eyes of Wesley Savitch and his hawk-faced brother.

"Nice evening," Savitch said casually.

"Not bad. Clouds are bunching up to the north," Ruff remarked.

Savitch glanced that way and nodded, "Uh-huh, might get some more rain."

"Savitch," Al said sharply, "are you helping or not? Why stand there jawing with the prisoners?"

"Why not?" Savitch replied. "We can be civilized."

"Sure. I'm always getting that stuff from Cavanaugh. Be civilized. You should see how civilized Jack Cavanaugh can be when he's worked up." He jabbed his rifle at Justice. "Let's go. Straight ahead. You can see the big house through the oaks. Follow your nose."

Ruff followed his nose.

The wind rattled the oaks and clouds slipped past before the stars. Emerging from the trees, they found the stone-and-log house. It was long and low, built in the shape of a U. There were lights in the windows, and around the house lounging men were smoking, drinking whiskey, muttering or breaking into laughter.

Ruff and the Englishmen were led up to the door through a covered passageway. The white-haired kid who carried enough guns to have a war with himself stood beside the door, his eyes challenging, waiting.

He probably hadn't killed anyone since noon and he was hungry for it.

Justice brushed past him and went in with Henry

and Oswald in his wake, Al and the Savitch brothers coming last.

"Right on through," Al said, and Ruff walked across the bare, scarred wooden floor to the far doorway, where light blazed and low conversation could be heard. Inside, General Jack Cavanaugh of the Army of the Undefeated sat at the head of his table flanked by two lovely women.

Laura York had been given a dress—one of Celia's, no doubt—and it fit her nicely. It was pale blue, subdued, a narrow collar of lace at the throat. Celia Landis, wore gold. Rings danced on her fingers, and her soft white hands fluttered here and there, landing frequently on Jack Cavanaugh's wrist.

Sir Henry swallowed an exclamation. Cavanaugh looked up.

"Come in, gentlemen, please be seated."

Ruff Justice seated himself next to Laura. She let her hand find his briefly beneath the table. She was scared, damned scared.

The table was nicely set—it should have been; Ruff recognized most of the pieces as Sir Henry's own. The rest of it was undoubtedly contraband as well.

"I'm happy you could all make it," Cavanaugh said, and he seemed to believe it himself momentarily—that he was a Southern gentleman with a charming wife, sitting down to dinner with a few chosen friends. "Especially Sir Henry and his brother—we have little opportunity to mingle with the nobility out here."

"Look here, Cavanaugh," Sir Henry began. He was leaning forward, his neck stretched out, eyes deep in his pale face. "I've had just about enough of this. Whatever it is you want, just take it and turn us loose."

Cavanaugh stared at him. Sir Henry had broken the spell. The Southern gentleman had become a plains pirate again, a butcher and a savage.

Celia patted his hand, quieting the madman as she sipped her golden wine. Ruff glanced around the room, seeing Donne, Al, and the Savitch brothers leaning against the bare walls. It seemed they didn't get to dine with the nobility.

There was a glassless window covered with oiled paper on the far wall. It would lead to the back of the house, but once a man was out there, there still wouldn't be anyplace to go.

"Wine, Sir Henry?" Cavanaugh asked, taking another stab at being a gentleman.

"No." Sir Henry could hardly speak. He was that angry.

"I . . ." Sir Oswald stuttered a little and finally got the wine poured for himself. He downed a lot of it very fast.

A couple of Chinese men in white suits appeared after a while, carrying silver platters—Sir Henry's platters, no doubt. The men never lifted their eyes.

"My servants," Cavanaugh said. "I took them from a railroad work gang. They've been adequate."

"For slaves," Ruff Justice said, and Cavanaugh's mad black eyes flickered to his.

"Yes." The man smiled after a moment. "For slaves."

"Is that what you're going to do with the soldiers you've taken prisoner?" Justice asked, cutting the pink roast beef he had been served.

"Make slaves of them?" Cavanaugh looked offended. "Of course not. They are warriors, as I am a warrior. They will be given the choice of joining my army or of being executed."

"You know a soldier in the U.S. army can't offer

his services to a private brigade," Justice said. "That doesn't leave them much choice, does it?"

Cavanaugh shrugged. He reached for the platter that had tinned smoked sturgeon on it and took half a pound. "I am happy to be the recipient of your larder," the madman told Sir Henry. "One grows tired of beef and more beef."

"Are you happy to be the recipient of my wife?" Sir Henry asked tightly.

"Of Celia and her affections—absolutely thrilled," Cavanaugh replied. He leaned over and squeezed Celia's arm, whispering something into her ear that made her blush. Justice realized that was more affection than he had ever seen Sir Henry give his wife.

"I ought to . . ." Sir Henry began. Cavanaugh's eyes came back to meet his and the lord fell silent.

"Ought to what?" Cavanaugh asked. His fist fell on the table suddenly, sending a platter flying. "Ought to what, Sir Henry? Kill me?" That thought caused Cavanaugh to pause, meditate, and then break into a deep laugh. "Ling! Clean up this mess," he shouted at the patient Chinese slave who stood by, towel over his arm.

"You'll never kill me, sir, not your type. You would kill me if I had hoof and horns and couldn't fight back, but you're no warrior. That's the difference between you and me—between you and a man like Justice." He studied Ruff now and then grunted with satisfaction or mild surprise. "Yes, he might try it, wouldn't you, Justice?"

"Not while you have all these gunhands around," Ruff said, placing another bite of meat in his mouth. He was the only one who was eating. Laura York sat rigid, hands clasped on her lap, and Sir Oswald and Celia were drinking. Sir Henry had drifted off into a silent, nearly motionless world.

"Alone? You and I?" Cavanaugh asked with interest. "Then would you try it?"

"Sure." Ruff swallowed, dabbed at his lips with one of Sir Henry's linen napkins, and put his knife and fork aside.

"With guns or knives?"

"With knives or bare knuckles or sticks or rocks," Justice told him, and Cavanaugh laughed again.

"I like you, Justice. You wouldn't want to join my army, would you?"

"Me?" Justice raised his eyebrows. "They only *say* that I'm mad."

That caused Cavanaugh to stiffen. He glared at Justice and for a minute Ruff thought he had gone too far. Then Jack Cavanaugh shifted his attention to Laura York, perhaps remembering that he needed to be on his best behavior.

"What was the name of your paper, Miss York?"

"The *Globe*. The *Climax Globe*."

"Ah. A daring editor was the man who hired you."

"He knows I do my job."

"Who does?" Cavanaugh demanded.

Ruff had to hand it to Laura York, she didn't miss a beat. "Tom Snelling. My editor."

Cavanaugh relaxed again. He was something to watch. Eyes shifting here and there, his body tensing, relaxing, his smile quickly giving way to rage.

"I know you've been covering the Landises' American tour, young lady, but I'll bet you never thought you'd come across a story this big."

"No, sir. No, sir, I didn't."

Cavanaugh was tying his napkin in a knot. "No, you couldn't have thought that. I need your newspaper, young lady. I am going to tell you the story of my life. I want it printed, every last detail of it just the way I dictate it."

"That's a lot of ink." Laura tried to keep her tone light, but Cavanaugh thundered.

"A lot of ink well used! What is it used on now? Corset advertisements, the results of the jelly-judging at the county fair, and lies. The lies of politicians. Every one of them is a liar. It hurts their mouths to speak the truth. Now I am going to tell you my life story, young lady, and you are going to see that it's printed. Sit back, all of you, and listen."

They didn't have much choice. Cavanaugh's captive audience sat back and listened. No one saw Ruff Justice slip the steak knife into his boot.

13

"I'm from Georgia," Jack Cavanaugh said, leaning back. "One day the government in Washington decided they had the right to murder us and burn our property if we didn't want Yankee rule. No matter that we'd seceded from the Union—we'd voluntarily joined it, so we figured we had the right to secede if we didn't like Washington rule and that jackanapes Republican, Mister Lincoln . . ."

There was no stopping Cavanaugh once he got started. He veered back and forth from his barefoot boyhood to his military career to his decision to fight on when "traitors" to the Confederacy like Robert E. Lee had surrendered.

Cavanaugh wandered down a lot of dusty Georgia roads and whirled through the houses of Congress, shooting at every random target. Verbally he refought the Civil War and won his own Western battle. He had found his biographer and he was going to make use of her.

Laura York interrupted. "Excuse me, can you tell me how you met Lady Celia?"

Sir Henry perked up. Sir Oswald poured another glass of wine. Cavanaugh smiled and took Celia's hand.

"I've known the lady for a long time. Before the

war, Lady Celia was a dancer with Emerald Sampson's troupe, and she toured America with that show. I met her in Atlanta one balmy night..."

He went on for a while in that vein. Ruff glanced at Donne and the Savitch brothers. They were grim, expressionless, even while Cavanaugh painted himself as a young man of sensitivity, a poet and romantic.

"Of course the war separated us. We corresponded regularly; Celia lived in England by then, having fled the advance of the Union cutthroats. She worked furiously for the Southern cause, gathering support for the Confederacy among the aristocracy."

Sir Henry said, "But by then we were together. I never knew—"

"How would you know anything!" Celia interrupted. "You knew nothing of British politics, let alone the problems of the American South. You cared about nothing but hunting. You were gone through most of the war. I had only Jack and his letters, and the Cause."

Cavanaugh gripped her hand quite tenderly. The two mad ones. It was all very touching.

"I myself made a visit to England to try to rally support," Cavanaugh said, "and it was then that we pledged our love forever—Celia and I. We are loyal to each other, loyal to the Cause. Eternally loyal."

"I wonder," Ruff Justice said, "what kind of bank balance you'd find if you could ever get back to England, Sir Henry?"

"Why—" He stared at his wife. "You married me to take my money and syphon it off to this thug."

Celia only smiled. "You wouldn't understand, Henry. This is more important than anything in your small world, more important than anything your narrow mind could conceive."

The Chinese slave came to take Ruff's plate and silver away. He hesitated fractionally, glanced at Ruff, and then hurriedly removed the dinner utensils. Minus the knife.

Laura York asked, "You robbed the bank in Climax?"

Celia didn't see any reason to hold back now, now that she was in her lover's fortress. "Of course. The more money, the longer, the better we fight."

Laura nearly broke then. She nearly hurled herself at the throat of the woman across the table, but Justice squeezed her knee, warning her.

"I met Jack secretly in Climax while we waited for Henry to organize his hunting party. We met and . . . we met. He told me that the bank was expecting a payroll and that I must hire two men, the Savitch brothers, and introduce them to Henry as bodyguards and rough country men. Jack had another project he had to take care of immediately—"

Ruff recalled that "project." A man in the small community of Willowbrush, Dakota Territory, had refused to shelter one of Jack Cavanaugh's men, and he had been caught and hung. Cavanaugh had gone back, burned down the town, and killed all but a handful of its inhabitants.

"I had never been involved in the war itself," Celia said.

"Understandable. It's been over for years," Ruff Justice put in.

The lady was unperturbed. "And so it was exciting for me to do what Jack had been doing for so long, to pick up a gun and fight for the freedom of the South."

Laura York could hardly restrain herself enough to ask her next question. "So you robbed the bank?"

"I did. Personally. In man's clothes, of course. I can't describe the sensation . . ."

She didn't have to. It was in her eyes. It had been enough, Justice thought, to cause her to dampen her pantaloons.

"And one of the people in that town," Laura York went on—Ruff could feel her knee trembling beneath his hand—"was killed."

"Only the banker," the lady said offhandedly.

"One of the Savitch brothers killed him."

"One of the Savitch brothers?" Lady Celia repeated. "No, dear. I did it myself, I'm the one who killed that banker, and I'm proud of it. Now I can call myself a soldier in Jack's army."

Laura York held herself back, but you could see it clearly in her eyes: the hatred, the wish to destroy. Celia and Jack Cavanaugh didn't seem to notice it. They were too busy gazing into each other's deranged eyes, making crazy promises.

"What are you going to do with me?" Sir Henry asked woodenly. They seemed to have forgotten he was there.

"Oh, we'll hold you for ransom. There's a chance someone in your family might want you and your brother back enough to pay for you."

"That might take months, years!"

"Possibly." Cavanaugh waved a hand. It was obviously of no importance to him one way or the other.

Justice figured that as soon as Laura York was out of sight, Henry and Oswald would be killed anyway. Why bother feeding a live hostage? A dead one was just as profitable.

"And Justice?" Laura York asked. As she did, Celia's eyes flickered to Ruff. The blonde smiled.

"I think Mister Justice can remain with us as well, don't you, Jack? It might help assure that Miss York prepares her story properly. You see, they are fond of each other." She sipped her wine, looking beauti-

127

ful, shiny, and hard in the lamplight. The diamond bracelet she wore gave off sparks as she gestured.

"Mister Justice will stay as well," Cavanaugh announced. "In the morning we can escort Miss York out of Indian territory, provide her with a horse, and await the results. You do have everything you need, Miss York?"

"Yes," she said quietly, her eyes still on Celia Landis, "I think so. Now I'd like to go back to my cabin and write out a brief sketch to fix it in my mind, so if you'll allow me to go?"

"An excellent idea." Cavanaugh rose. "But first let me show you something. A surprise. Celia?"

She too rose.

Ruff got up as well, seeing the Savitch brothers, Donne, and Al straighten and start toward the door. A lot of good that little sausage knife was going to do him. Cavanaugh had more guards than the King of England.

Justice held Laura's chair as she got up, holding her skirt out of the way. "You did fine," he whispered.

"Scared to death."

"I know. Just keep it up."

"That bitch! I could kill her."

"Try to take it easy. Remember you're a newspaperwoman."

Cavanaugh called over his shoulder. "Come along, hurry up. Celia has something to show us."

Ruff took Laura's arm and they went out the door past the pale-haired moron who stood guard. They started off through the trees toward the wagons. The moon was high and bright, the clouds built towers among the stars. The oaks were gesturing black giants in the wind.

They arrived at the wagon train, Cavanaugh still jovial, Celia clinging to his arm, while Sir Henry wandered along in a daze behind them. Sir Oswald was having trouble walking. Justice used the time to try to find holes in the defenses of Cavanaugh's army. Where would guards be posted, where wouldn't they be? And once off the mountain, where could a man go? That was the hardest question.

Justice figured it was worth a try, however, as soon as Laura was gone, assuming Cavanaugh didn't change his mind about that part of the bargain.

"Where, dear?" Cavanaugh asked.

Celia Landis took a lantern from one of Cavanaugh's henchmen and hung it on the side of the wagon. Then with a smile she bent down and removed the false bottom to the water barrel.

She reached in and went suddenly pale, searching frantically for a moment before she could murmur, "Gone."

"What?" Cavanaugh leapt forward.

"The money. It's gone."

"But it has to be here. I need it, Celia!" Cavanaugh's voice was booming. Celia looked more than a little shaken. "I had a reason for having you rob that bank. I'm short of cash. I've got a payroll to meet."

"You mean these boys would take money to fight for the Cause?" Ruff Justice asked. Avery Donne kicked him savagely behind the knee and Justice fell on his face.

"You shut your mouth, Justice."

"Enough, Avery," Cavanaugh said. "Celia—where is that money, dammit!"

Justice got slowly to his feet. Laura looked at him with concern. He shook his head. He was all right. Cavanaugh had started to tear the water barrel apart. It was cleverly made: the bottom ten inches were hollow and the top thirty inches weren't.

As Cavanaugh yanked and tore at the barrel staves, the barrel burst open. Water flooded out, drenching the outlaw. Cavanaugh fell back cursing. Someone laughed, and that did it.

Cavanaugh whipped out a pistol and shot into the barrel, kicking at it, ripping it apart stave by stave, cursing and screaming as he did so. Justice took Laura's arm and backed away very carefully. Donne was looking at them with cold eyes, but Wesley Savitch shot Justice an amused glance. Celia just stood staring as her hero, the revolutionary leader, the man of her dreams, went utterly berserk. Bloodying his hands as he ripped at the wood, Cavanaugh emptied his pistol into the barrel and then hurled his gun at what was left of it, slipping once in the mud so that he fell to his knee.

He rose heavily and said hoarsely to Donne, "Find it. There's twenty-five thousand dollars in paper money missing. You find it, Avery."

Then he turned and stamped away, pushing past Justice before disappearing into the trees. Celia Landis just stared.

Now she knew.

"You just stay put," Avery said to Ruff.

"I've got nowhere to go."

"You're right there, scout. *You* don't know where that money got to, do you?"

"Not me," Justice answered. But he thought he knew who did. A glance at Laura York told him he was right. "Will they find it?" he asked in an undertone.

"I don't think so," she answered.

"I thought you weren't going to do any more snooping around the wagons."

"Only a little. Enough to find the money. I just got it hidden when Cavanaugh attacked us."

The men had begun to tear the wagons apart plank by plank. Ruff glanced around casually. Wesley Savitch and Al were still watching. They hadn't forgotten Ruff during the excitement.

Ruff walked to where Savitch stood. The gunman's hand went to his holster. Ruff stopped a healthy distance away. "This is some outfit you've hooked up with."

"It pays."

"Does it? What happens if it doesn't pay, if they don't find that cash?"

Wesley Savitch shrugged. Someone ripped the table out of Sir Henry's wagon and threw it out the back. "I drift," Savitch said. "Me and Rafer, we're businessmen."

"Suppose Cavanaugh doesn't want you drifting?"

"Then he's got a problem," Savitch said.

"What are you two talking about?" Avery Donne called across the clearing.

"The weather," Savitch answered. He wasn't very easily intimidated. As if to add authenticity to Savitch's reply, thunder rumbled in from the north and the wind began to blow harder.

Ruff looked at the sky. Maybe under the cover of a storm . . . it was just about impossible. He would need to take Laura with him, to find two horses, to cross more than a hundred miles of plains. And what about Henry and Oswald? What about the cavalrymen who were locked up somewhere? It wasn't too likely a plan; still Ruff welcomed the storm as the first drops began to fall, the clouds closing up the gap where the moon had shone.

Returning to where Laura stood, he watched them unloading the wagons. They had gotten to the freight wagons now. Buffalo hides and trophy heads, crates of food and ammunition, tents and firewood, littered the ground. Ruff looked at Laura and she shook her head.

"Not yet."

"Have they gone by it?" he asked.

The redhead smiled. "That's right," she answered. "They've missed it again."

"Laura, I want you to promise me you won't antagonize Cavanaugh or argue with him. Just do as he asks, and when he sends you back, you go."

"Without you?"

"Without me. It's your best, maybe your only chance. You'll be safe. Whoever he sends with you will be under orders not to touch you. Cavanaugh wants the publicity of a newspaper story. He wants some kind of legitimacy and he thinks you can give it to him. Deep down, Cavanaugh knows he's nothing but a murderer and a thief."

"I won't leave you, Ruffin," she said, turning toward him.

The rain fell in scattered, huge drops. The wind shifted her dress, her hair.

"You'll leave me—if it means you get out of here alive," Ruff insisted.

"And you . . ."

"I'll get out." Ruff Justice looked up at the storm. "I'll get out of here, Laura. You can bet on it."

As Laura clung briefly to him, Justice wondered if he had ever made a hollower boast.

The wagons were searched and searched again. They stayed there until midnight, watching Cavanaugh's people dismantle the wagons. Then the rain drove them off. The search would have to wait until morning.

"Maybe one of 'em's got it on him," Avery Donne said to Wesley Savitch. He was looking at Laura when he said it. "Maybe we ought to search them."

"No need to," Savitch said. "Twenty-five thousand would make a bulge you could see a mile away. It's not on 'em."

Avery Donne appeared miffed. He had wanted to do some searching. There weren't many women out this way, damn few that looked like Laura York.

"You'll have to ask Cavanaugh before you start something like that," Savitch said.

"Who asked you? Where'd you come from anyway?"

"The lady hired me and my brother. And what the lady wants she gets. She wants me to keep the lid on."

Donne had an answer, but all that Justice heard was a hiss, like the sound the rain made falling through the oaks. Then the man turned and stalked away, Al on his heels. Good, Justice thought, a rift in the outlaw band. Donne saw himself as Cavanaugh's lieutenant, but Celia had brought her own man along. The word was sure to spread quickly that the expected payroll hadn't shown up. These people were all mercenaries, every single one of them. Only Cavanaugh believed in the Cause. Cavanaugh and maybe a few other insane soldiers.

Like the pale-haired kid.

He was there now, appearing out of nowhere. Savitch glanced at the kid, the three-gun moron.

"Cavanaugh says tuck 'em in. It's rainin'," the kid said. He seemed to think it was the funniest joke ever told; he broke into a cracked little laugh.

Savitch's eyes were cold. Rain dripped from his dark hat brim. The kid saw something he didn't like in Savitch's eyes and he quit laughing. He quit laughing and rested each hand on a holstered gun. His lip curled back and his shoulders hunched forward expectantly.

"Put 'em away, then," Savtich said, turning his back disdainfully. He walked away, leaving the kid to stand there looking a little foolish as he prepared to draw his weapons, to kill.

He wouldn't forget that moment. The kid was an idiot, but he was smart enough to know when he had been slighted.

And he was smart enough to pull a trigger.

"Let's go," the pale-haired kid shouted, and Ruff moved—immediately. The kid was ready to shoot and didn't care who or what it was. Ruff touched Laura's arm and then walked away, followed by the wild-eyed kid.

Laura, Ruff saw, was taken to a small cabin near the horse corral where fifty or seventy-five of the fastest horses in the West—outlaws' horses—stood in the rain.

That was all he saw. Cavanaugh's thugs pushed him and the Englishmen into their cabin and locked the door. There was no light at all, only the troubled breathing of Sir Oswald, the drumming of the rain on the roof.

Sir Henry Landis lay down on his bunk and there was a small, forlorn sound, a sound like a child crying. Ruff looked away, even though no one could see him in the darkness. There are times when a man cries, but he doesn't cry out of cowardice. Not if he wants to remain a man.

"Rest for a while," Justice told them both.

"How can we rest?" Sir Oswald asked.

"Do it. We're leaving this place."

The silence was a vast dark question. Oswald voiced it. "How? How can we do that, Justice? Why, all we have to do is remain, endure. Maybe it will take some time for Cavanaugh to get his ransom. But all we have to do is—"

"All you have to do is die," Ruff said sharply. "He'll never let you out of here alive."

"But why?"

"Why? Because he doesn't need to keep you alive. Your relatives will be informed that you're here, that they have to send a ransom. They will or they won't, I don't know how they feel about you, but Cavanaugh doesn't want to feed you or guard you for all that while. So he'll bury you."

Sir Henry sobbed again.

"He wouldn't dare," Sir Oswald said almost desperately.

"This man," Justice told them, "would dare anything. He's fighting a holy war. As soon as Laura York is gone, our protection is gone. He won't kill us in front of her; he wants his image untarnished. But after she's gone . . ." Ruff shrugged in the darkness. The rain pounded down.

"How can we . . ." Henry Landis managed to whisper. "How can we possibly escape?"

"I don't know," Justice said. "Maybe we can't. Maybe it's a pipe dream of mine, but either we try it or wait here to be slaughtered like lambs."

"I can't . . ." Sir Henry said. It sounded as if he was talking into his pillow.

"Then don't." Justice's voice grew angry. "Stay here, damn you. Stay and die. I'm going tonight. If you don't want to live, stay where you are, keep on crying. If you want to be a man, you get up on your feet and let's have a go at it. I don't want to drag you along, Landis. Believe me, my chances are much better without you and your brother. But you've got to make up your mind. Crawl or fight, because I'm going. Tonight."

It was a long time before Sir Henry answered. Ruff saw him sit up, paw at his eyes, and heard his voice, tense and angry. "We're going. You're not the only warrior in this room," he said. "I've been places you've never dreamed of, faced tigers and Cape buffalo. I've got the blood of conquerors in my veins, Justice. And believe it or not, so does Oswald."

Ruff didn't answer. What was there to say? The blood of his ancestors wasn't going to help Landis now. The best he could do was try to avoid spilling any. Before the night was over someone would bleed. Someone was sure to die.

The rain fell and the thunder rumbled outside the cabin walls. Ruff Justice rolled up in the thin, lousy blanket to try to rest, to try to sleep before the war began.

14

The minutes dripped past like the rainwater trickling from the eaves. Ruff Justice lay looking at the dark ceiling, listening to Sir Oswald's heavy breathing, Sir Henry's occasional whimper. He lay there and tried to total up their chances of escaping from the outlaw stronghold. He kept coming up with the same number, something less than zero.

The trouble was their chances of surviving here were even less than that. Cavanaugh would kill them all the minute Laura York had gone on her way to write up the exploits and life of the famous General Jack Cavanaugh.

Ruff's fingers closed around the carving knife he had lifted from the general's table. It wasn't going to be of much use, but it was something.

Justice sat up and Sir Henry gasped.

"What is it?" the nobleman hissed.

"We're going. There's no point in waiting."

"They'll kill us if they see us," Sir Henry said.

Justice didn't bother to answer. Crossing the room to the sleeping bulk of Sir Oswald, he shook the fat man awake, feeling the soft muscles, his total unsuitability for an escapade like this. It was just one more thing that couldn't be helped. They would try it together. No one would be left behind.

Sir Henry had risen from the cot. He stood beside Justice, hunched forward, panting through his nose. The blood in his body was racing three to four times its normal speed. His lungs gasped for air as if he were preparing to run. His body knew danger was afoot.

"Time, is it?" Sir Oswald asked, rolling to his feet.

"It's time."

"Well," the Englishman said, "this is a moment of truth, isn't it? No chance, Justice?"

"Always a chance."

"Good. Nice to hear that." Sir Oswald's voice was actually cheerful, strained but cheerful. Perhaps the man had unsuspected depths.

"What are we going to do?" Sir Henry asked. In the darkness Ruff could feel the animal tension.

"Get out of here. Out of this cabin and then to the horses and Miss York's cabin. If we make it that far, we'll try to figure out some way to get to Sergeant Cairot and his people in the big bunkhouse. The rain and the darkness are going to help us out. We should be able to make a run for it."

"First," Sir Oswald reminded Ruff patiently, "we should find some way out of this cabin."

Ruff smiled grimly in the darkness. "Easy. We break down the door."

"What?" Sir Henry was incredulous. "What are you talking about?"

"Listen to me. It's not a very good plan, but it's all I have, Landis. One of you is going to have to kill a man with naked steel. Which one?"

There was a long silence before Sir Oswald said, "I'll try. How?"

"If you don't know what you're doing, go for the throat. I'm going to get that guard in here by making just a little too much noise. I think it's safe to assume that I'm the one they're worried about, if they're worried at all. That leaves it up to you."

"With the knife?"

"The knife," Ruff said, and he placed the handle in Sir Oswald's hand.

"What if I botch this?" the Englishman asked.

"Then it's over. You've bled game? Do the same thing, only don't be tentative. Get him."

"And if there's more than one guard?" Sir Henry asked. "If there's three or four . . ."

Justice didn't have an answer. It didn't do to think too far ahead. That would mean surrendering to the inevitable failure.

"Let's try it and see." He looked at his unlikely allies in the darkness. "Unless you gentlemen want to sleep until the executioner comes."

"Let's try it," Sir Oswald said in a gravelly voice. Sir Henry stepped aside while Sir Oswald took a position behind the door. Ruff Justice positioned himself on the wall between two cots and began slowly thumping on the logs. That should bring someone to see what was up. Maybe.

Ruff kicked at the logs, feeling his own heart thumping harder now, as he watched the door anxiously, seeing only the thin glint of light from the blade of Sir Oswald's knife.

It might have been five minutes or ten before the diversion finally had its effect. Ruff heard a boot on the low step of the cabin and his breath caught. He kicked furiously at the cabin wall. There was a moment's grumbling outside and then the door opened.

It was Avery Donne himself. Water dripped from his black slicker, from the brim of his black hat. He had a rifle in his hands and a malicious gleam in his eyes. Outside, a storm lantern illuminated the front of the cabin.

"Is that the best you could come up with, Justice?" Donne sneered. "From all the stories they tell about you I thought you'd have a bagful of tricks."

Ruff's eyes seemed to be on Donne, but they weren't. He was watching the man behind the outlaw, the pudgy man with the knife in his hand, the man who stood there, frozen.

Move, damn you! Ruff shouted silently, trying not to let his eyes give him away. Move.

Still Sir Oswald remained fixed, bent slightly forward, his forehead glistening with sweat.

"Get up, Justice," Donne said coldly. "I guess I'm going to have to teach you something."

Move!

Finally Sir Oswald did. The creak of the floorboards caused Avery Donne to turn his head slightly. Sir Oswald launched himself at the outlaw. Quick, it had to be quick. If Donne pulled the trigger of that Winchester, the game was over.

Sir Oswald had moved with desperate speed, his eyes wide with fear, mouth pursed with determination. He had once stepped in to bleed a Bengal tiger Sir Henry had shot, as it lay there twitching, possibly alive. He had put steel to the animal's throat just as its amazingly powerful body shook off the effect of a bullet and began to respond. To have that thing come alive under you, to see yellow eyes and fangs was something you don't forget, something you wouldn't want to repeat in a lifetime.

Sir Oswald was finding it repeated now.

This time the tiger was a man, as violent and deadly as the big cat. It had to be done, and so Sir Oswald did it. Knife found flesh and hot blood spewed from the artery in Avery Donne's throat as Sir Oswald slashed across the soft flesh.

Ruff lunged forward and ripped the gun from Donne's hands before a reflexive movement of a finger could bring death to all of them. Sir Henry was on his feet, shocked, looking primitive and ineffective all at once.

Sir Oswald stood puffing, blood smearing his clothes, the bloody knife in hands.

"That was murder..."

"The hell it was," Justice said. Maybe in London it would have been. Here it was survival, nothing more. "Let's go, come on," he hissed. They could see the rain slanting down steadily outside. The storm lantern swung in the breeze.

Ruff had to practically push Sir Henry toward the door. He handed him the Winchester. No matter what kind of man he was, Sir Henry knew where to put the sights of a rifle.

Justice took Donne's handgun from its holster, stepped across the body, and went out into the stormy night.

The first three steps were the ones that tugged at the heart, dried the mouth, lifted the pulse to a whining in the ears. They didn't know who was out there, how many of them. They just went out, taking the only chance they had.

Justice pulled the door shut behind them and latched it. "Leave the lantern," he whispered to Sir Oswald, who had reached for it.

"I can't see a damn thing."

"Neither can they," Ruff said. "Come on. Let's get Miss York."

Get Laura and get the hell out of here. Leave Cavanaugh to his madness and his murder. Ruff was running toward the girl's cabin, his feet silent against the sodden earth, his hair in his eyes as the rain drove down. The outlaw stepped out from behind the oak tree and Ruff just kept going.

Whether the man ever saw him as more than a moving shadow in the night Justice didn't know. He lowered his shoulder and the two men went down in a heap, Ruff's gun barrel slashing out to thud against the outlaw's skull.

When Justice rose, he was alone.

He yanked off the man's slicker and hat and waited a few seconds for Sir Oswald to arrive, Sir Henry on his heels. Sir Oswald stopped short, hesitated, and then continued, finally recognizing Ruff.

"Who's that?" Sir Henry asked in a whisper.

"No idea. Oswald, the knife."

"I can't," the nobleman said, "not again."

"Give it to me."

Sir Oswald did so and Ruff bent to finish the job. It was simple butchery, but the Englishman couldn't know how many innocent people these thugs of Cavanaugh had slaughtered. Sometimes for the mere entertainment of it.

"Wait here," Justice ordered the Englishmen when he was finished.

"I can help..."

"I don't want your help. Not now. One man is quieter, less visible. Wait here!"

There was no more argument. Ruff turned and kept going, the rain hammering down, racketing through the trees. There was a light on in the cabin where Laura York was being held, and the door was open.

Ruff frowned. That made no sense. In another minute it did make sense as Justice heard her muted cry for help, heard distinctly the sound of a slap, a callused hand meeting flesh.

There was a fury in Justice now, a reckless anger, and he ran on, watching as the door to the cabin was closed, shutting out the light. But for a brief moment Justice saw the interior of the cabin, saw Laura York sprawled on the floor, saw Al turn toward the door and shut it. Al, his single eye gleaming, his whiskered, battered face twisted with carnal expectations.

Ruff Justice hit the door with his shoulder just as Al dropped his pants. The door was solid, but Ruff burst through it, rolling to the floor and then coming to his feet to throw himself at Al, his hand with the pistol in it slashing at the bandit's face.

Al screamed as his nose was smashed. Blood spattered the room and Laura, her hand to her mouth, eyes wide with dread, scooted into a corner.

Al tried to draw his gun from his holster but he didn't even come close. He was on his knees now, his face smeared with gore. Justice kicked him full in the face and Al's neck cracked sickeningly as he was hurled back to lie still against the planks of the cabin floor.

"Ruff, I . . ." Laura reached out for him, but Justice's eyes were on the door.

"Get up, let's go!"

"Yes." She was hurt, briefly, but she was woman enough to realize that Ruff couldn't stand there explaining, petting her just then. She was dressed quickly, glancing only once toward the bloodied thing on the floor.

"What now?" Laura asked. She was flushed, beautiful.

"Get you on a horse and get you out of here," Ruff answered. "You and my two friends."

"What two friends?"

Ruff told her. Laura shook her head. "And then what are you going to do, Justice?"

"Try to get those army personnel free."

"You push it as far as it goes, don't you?" the redhead asked.

"Can't leave 'em. There's one other thing, Laura."

"What?"

"The money."

"The bank money? This is no time to worry about that, Ruff," she said.

"Sure it is. Didn't you notice how the loss of the money started to pull the gang apart? Savitch wouldn't be here, wouldn't fight for Cavanaugh if it weren't for the promise of a big payday. There's got to be a lot of other men who feel the same way. You don't sit out in the wilderness eating out of tin cans for month after month with no promise of reward. Money is what holds any bunch of crooks together; it's what's holding Jack Cavanaugh's bunch here."

"All right." Laura took a deep breath. She glanced toward the door. No one had shown up yet. Al had been careful to send everyone away so he could play. "You're probably right. I haven't been thinking too well. I only know I'm scared to death, Ruffin."

"Where is the money?"

"Inside a buffalo head. The big bull that Sir Henry shot first. When they were searching the wagon, they just threw it outside. Put your hand in the back of the head. There's a buckskin purse in there. The twenty-five thousand is inside. We can—"

"*You* can do what I told you. Get on a horse and ride."

Her eyes sparked. "That's safer, is it?"

"Maybe. I hope so." He took her by the shoulders briefly. "I need to be alone, to move around silently."

"All right." She shrugged. "You're the boss, you're the warrior. What do I do?"

"Get to the corral. Henry and Oswald are out in the oaks waiting. Get three horses—haze out any others you can without making a fuss—and ride."

"Toward Lincoln and—"

"West. Ride west."

"Away from the fort."

"It's your best chance. The rain will cover your tracks, and if you stay in the hills, you might make it. Circle back toward the place where I killed the Indian. The place we made love. You recall it?"

She looked at him and smiled softly. "What do you think?" On tiptoes she kissed him and then was gone, out the door and into the rainy night. She was something, Laura York: a good soldier, a woman.

Ruff turned and went out.

He stayed hunched in the shadows, watching for Cavanaugh's soldiers as Laura and the Englishmen slipped out of the corral with their horses. When they were on their way, sending a few of the outlaws' horses ahead of them, Ruff rose and started on again.

It wasn't going to be this easy at the barracks where the soldiers were being kept prisoner.

Justice saw five men walking their slow rounds in the rain. Cavanaugh had reasoned that if there were trouble, it would come from a barracks full of cavalrymen and not from a handful of civilians.

The rain still fell and darkness covered Ruff's movements, but sooner or later someone would discover the body of Avery Donne, discover that the prisoners had escaped. There just wasn't much time.

The odds looked lousy, but it hadn't been a night for the odds. If nothing else worked, at least Justice knew he had given Laura a chance to survive and had given freedom to the Englishmen. His good luck couldn't run forever, but he could try. The army was paying him, and they had a right to expect service.

Ruff Justice tugged down his hat and moved forward through the desolate night.

15

Ruff Justice had watched them for long enough. Long enough to know the routines of the guards. Like all soldiers forced to walk a repetitious, boring round under uncomfortable circumstances, they had fallen into patterns; like all such guards, they were less than alert now as the hours passed, as the rain drove down. They turned their faces down, trudged back and forth, and waited for their relief.

Some of them would never see that relief come.

Ruff Justice walked forward at a steady pace, his own head bowed. Reaching the corner of the long log bunkhouse, he paused, looked behind him, and then stood waiting while the guard on that side walked slowly toward him, slogging through the rain and mud.

"What the hell?" the guard began truculently.

Ruff fed his fantasies. "They said to come over and get a cup of coffee."

"Damn near time," the man said with relief. He lowered his rifle and Ruff slammed his gun butt against the side of the outlaw's face. He sighed and went down. Ruff looked left and then right. He dragged the thug into the trees and quickly bound and gagged him with his own belt and bandanna. Snatching up the man's weapon, he sprinted back to the log cabin, reaching his victim's post just as a second guard rounded the corner.

"Screw this," the new arrival muttered, lighting a smoke.

"It'd be all right if they paid us," Justice said.

"Shit, I haven't been paid ..." It reached the guard's brain finally. "Who the hell are you!"

Justice swung the Winchester like a club and the guard went down heavily, his cigarette snuffed out as it touched the muddy earth. Ruff dragged him away to join his friend.

The storm clouds had begun to thin, the rain to lighten. Now, briefly, the moon broke through the silver clouds and Ruff grumbled a curse. This wasn't the sort of help he needed for this night's work.

Ruff was gathering quite a collection of weapons; now what he needed was some soldiers to use them.

Getting the boys out of that cabin still wasn't going to be easy. The odds were a little better, but they weren't going to let Justice walk up to the front door and let the cavalrymen out.

Walking the guard's round, Ruff studied the windows along that side of the barracks. They didn't look all that tough: boarded up haphazardly, with light seeping through. He paused, looking up.

"What's the matter?"

At the sound of the voice Justice lowered his eyes and turned away to cough into his fist.

"Thought somebody was at the window," Justice muttered, and the other man came nearer.

"Don't see nothin'."

"Looks like the boards are loose on that side," Ruff pointed out. The man stretched up to look and Justice cold-cocked him as well.

"I should have been a mugger," Ruff grumbled as he dragged his third victim into the trees. Everything was going well, almost too well, but Justice

147

wasn't taken in by it. He wasn't going to mug fifty Cavanaugh outlaws. He wasn't going to sneak the four remaining soldiers and Sir Henry's six servants out of there without the whole mountain going up like a powder keg.

Justice went back to the cabin. Thrusting the barrel of his captured Winchester beneath a loosely nailed plank, he pried and the board came away from the window frame with a shriek.

Ruff looked around, pried a second board loose, and then ripped them free. He chinned himself and looked in the window. The prisoners lay on the floor wrapped in blankets. There was no guard inside. A lantern burned low on each wall.

Justice tapped on the glass pane. He tapped only twice, and someone, unable to sleep as a prisoner, rolled over and glanced up.

Reb Saunders grinned and slipped from his blanket. He limped heavily and there was a knot above his eyes. He saw Ruff, nodded, and glanced toward the door. Then cautiously he came to the window.

Ruff gestured what he intended to do with Saunders' help. The soldier returned to his bed, brought the blanket to the window, and held it up to the glass. Ruff rapped the pane with his gun butt and the glass, muffled by the blanket, fell inward.

"Mister Justice, damn all! I should've known if there was a way out of this—"

"Wake everybody up," Justice said impatiently. "Keep 'em quiet."

"We're goin'?"

"We're going. Make it fast, Reb." Then Justice winked and handed the corporal a Colt .44-40 revolver. Reb Saunders took the weapon like a holy relic, winked back, and slid inside, tucking his new treasure into his belt. Swiftly and quietly, he told

148

the others what was up, and one by one they moved to the window.

Wadie Cairot managed to look bitterly angry, even with his uniform torn and his head bloodied. He glowered at Justice.

"Let's go," Justice hissed, and Wadie, with a boost from two soldiers, came up and over. The NCO stood beside Ruff and he was trembling, not from the cold or from fear—no, not Wadie Cairot—but with emotion. He couldn't forget, couldn't let go of his anger for Justice. He lumped Cavanaugh and his crimes and Justice and his indiscretions in the same pile.

"Move," Ruff said. "Twenty paces back you'll find some men tied up. There's a rifle or two as well."

Then Justice helped Billy Sondberg over, sent him after Cairot with a slap on the rump, and helped the next man down.

One of them—they called him Fritz—was badly wounded. It didn't look good for him, but he would go along. He had little choice.

It did give Ruff a moment's thought, however. The larger his army got, the more liabilities he was carrying along. Henry and Oswald. Cairot. The badly wounded Fritz.

"Well?" Cairot was back, gripping a Winchester tightly. He was grudgingly giving Justice command for the time being, and it was galling.

"The other prisoners have to be gotten out. The English servants, the trail hands. Hawk."

"We can handle that," Cairot said.

"Can you? It has to be quiet. Dead quiet."

"What do you think I am, Justice," Cairot said, his voice rising in pitch, "some kind of fool?"

Ruff didn't answer for a long moment.

"Finish up the guards," he said at last. "Quietly. The horses are through the trees there. The canyon where Sir Henry went after cougar is where we want to go. Can you find that?"

"We can find it," Wadie Cairot said, "but why there? We've got to strike out for the fort."

"There's no chance that way, Wadie."

"It's the shortest line."

Ruff played a trump. "I've sent Sir Henry and his brother and Laura York to the canyon."

Wadie stared at Ruff for a long moment in the rain. Then he nodded. Cairot wasn't real imaginative, but he was steadfast. The colonel had said to watch the Englishmen. He would watch them. If they'd gone to the canyon, he would go.

"All right," Cairot growled. "If we can get out of here alive, we'll head that way. What about you, Justice? Aren't you coming?"

"I've got something else to do, Cairot." Something important. Something that just might have a crippling effect on Jack Cavanaugh's army.

The money.

"Get, now," Ruff whispered. "I'll try to catch up." He fell silent. There was a dark figure moving toward them, one of the two remaining guards. He moved nervously, slowly, but they saw him relax and stride forward.

"There you are," he said with relief. "I was getting antsy. Couldn't figure out where in hell—"

That was as far as he got. Reb Saunders had moved toward him, and before the guard could recognize the army uniform, it was too late for him. He'd never recognize anything or anybody again.

Ruff stepped up beside Reb, whose shoulders were heaving with emotion.

"They killed eight of us, Ruffin T. Eight good men. Friends of mine."

"I know they did," Justice said.

"They have to pay, don't they?"

150

"That's right. They have to pay."

"What is this, a wake?" Wadie Cairot demanded. "Let's get moving."

"Get the prisoners and get out," Ruff said. "Luck to you, boys."

"And to you, Mister Justice," Billy Sondberg whispered as the tall man in buckskins filtered off through the shadows and the rain.

Justice didn't hear Billy's last words. His mind was occupied with other things. His ears and eyes were already searching for the enemy.

He found the wagon train easily. Sir Henry's equipment, trophies, sections of the wagons themselves were still strewn across the ground.

A guard, he thought. There would have to be a guard, but he saw none. And then he did. Frowning, Justice moved closer, making sure.

The man in the rain slicker lay on his side, one wide open, white eye staring up at the shifting clouds. His throat had been opened up for him. Very neatly.

Ruff's eyes narrowed. Crouching, he looked around, seeing no one else. And then he saw her.

She was going through the hides and antlers when her movements seem to indicate sudden knowledge. She moved forward on her knees, arms extended almost pleadingly as her hands slipped inside the head of the big bull buffalo.

Ruff Justice watched her. He walked up behind Lady Celia, the dancer, and she didn't hear him, didn't see him.

She drew the buckskin sack from the buffalo head and opened it with trembling fingers. Ruff saw her withdraw a sheaf of bills from the sack. He recognized the paper band around them.

"Bank of Climax," he said quietly, and she spun around, reaching inside her jacket.

Ruff Justice let her have a short right-hand shot

to the jaw and she sagged to the ground, to lie in the rain. He lifted the buckskin sack, stuffed the bills from her hand back into it, and tucked it inside his shirt. Then he opened Celia's jacket and took the bloody knife from it. It was Ruff's own skinning knife. He was happy to see it again, sorry to see it had been used so brutally, used to kill for profit. She had cut the guard's throat with that razor-edged little blade—and what was the woman in this for now? He had taken her for a bored wife, a woman who needed some romance, even violent romance in her life—but now, it seemed, she had turned her back on Cavanaugh. Maybe Jack's tantrum of the evening before had made her decide to just take the money and run.

She wouldn't be running far alone.

The shots from across the camp split the night and Ruff looked up, a savage expression twisting his mouth. Something had gone wrong. Cairot hadn't handled it right and now the game was up.

Ruff scooped up the woman at his feet and slung her over his shoulder. And then he was running for the corral, running, and when one of Cavanaugh's men appeared suddenly before him, Justice shot him in the face. He was blown back to die against the black oak tree.

That did it.

From somewhere in the trees another rifle opened up. Someone was trying to sting Justice with searing hot lead. A .44 bullet whined off the oak tree beside Justice and disappeared into the dark of the storm, spattering him with bark.

The Cavanaugh soldiers had been roused and now they had found their targets.

Ruff nearly ran into another man, this one moving away from him. He was creeping forward, rifle in hands, hatless, the rain glossing his slicker. Ruff stopped short and realized the the man hadn't seen him. He crept on, looking right and left. Justice watched him go.

Ruff took a minute to shift Celia's weight and started on again. The horses were suddenly before him, wandering in confusion, some of them rearing up in fright as a gun report sounded and simultaneous lightning scarred the sky. Where Cairot was Ruff didn't know. The element of surprise had been lost, obviously, but maybe the NCO had managed to pull it off.

Justice hoped so for the sake of Saunders, Billy Sondberg and Hawk. Even for the sake of those Englishmen and trail hands who were caught up in this madness through no fault of their own, who would die without reason if Cairot had blown it completely.

Justice had to go back and try to help out. He had Celia and the money. He had Laura York and the noble lords ahead of him, all them helpless in the wilderness, all of them marked for death.

Justice caught up with a dun horse that still wore saddle and bridle. He couldn't tell much about the animal in the darkness, but it would have to do even if it was running on three legs.

He threw Celia up and over the withers and swung aboard.

"Justice!"

Ruff turned and ducked, firing even as the voice called out. He knew who it was, knew it was no friend of his.

Rafer Savitch's bullet whipped past Ruff's head as the dun horse danced away. Justice saw the outlaw's face by lightning, the twisted sneer of his mouth. Ruff had no pity at all for Rafer Savitch. He had come to kill for pay.

Let him die for pay.

Ruff's first bullet did the job, although he kept firing. The first bullet tagged Rafer Savitch's skull and exploded the outlaw's skull like a ripe melon. The gun dropped from Rafer's nerveless hand, but a pointing finger remained, a finger that jabbed at Justice as Rafer Savitch, dead from the moment of impact, fell over into the mud.

Justice rode the dun out toward the gate and emptied his gun into the air, driving many of the remaining horses before him.

Another bandit appeared briefly from the trees and fired half a dozen times, but none of the shots was very close, and Ruff, ducking low, whipped the dun away from the fire and into the darkness of the empty hills.

After half a mile he slowed. He pulled the excited horse to the side of the trail and watched his backtrail. He could see nothing nearby; in the distance there was fire. The outlaw bunkhouses and possibly the big house had been set on fire. One of Wadie's ideas? If so, it was a good one. Burn the place to the ground.

Maybe that's what brought them running so fast, Justice wondered. He would have to wait until he saw one of the soldiers before he could be certain.

Assuming he ever saw any of them again at all.

There was no guarantee of that, none that Ruff himself would survive this night. He looked at the woman across his horse's withers: her outflung arm, her tangled, long blond hair. It was difficult to keep himself from slapping her unconscious face, to keep from dumping her in the brush. She was a killing thing, one of those who killed out of ignorance and mistaken ideals, caring nothing for anyone else's life. She had caused a lot of blood to flow and it wasn't over yet.

Ruff touched her yellow hair gently and rode on.

16

Morning was bright and cold. Freshets silvered the bottom of the badlands, stretching out for mile upon mile. On the ledge where the cold wind raked his long dark hair Ruff Justice crouched, looking out at his backtrail.

The blonde stirred, moaned, and sat up.

Ruff Justice turned and walked to her, standing over Celia until she was fully awake, staring at Justice with venom in her eyes.

"What's happened?" she asked.

"We're running."

"Running!" She tried to get to her feet, failed, and plopped back down. "I've got to get to Jack Cavanaugh."

"Why?"

"Why!" Her wide green eyes opened wider. "If I don't, he'll—"

"Kill you, but he's going to kill you anyway, isn't he, Celia? You've crossed him now."

"I didn't . . ." She tried to act indignant but it didn't quite come off.

"You did. You slipped off on your own to look for that money. You cut one of Cavanaugh's men's throats. You think he'll trust you again?"

"I don't care," she said hoarsely, her head hanging. Now she looked up and her eyes flashed a warning. "I'd kill again."

"I bet you would, darling," Ruff said quietly. "What happened, though? What made you want to cut and run?"

"Did you see him?" Celia came to her feet in one rapid movement. She stood rubbing her eyes, staring at the surrounding hills. "He's mad!"

"No fooling," Ruff said sardonically.

"I didn't know that. How could I know? I've never seen anything like that. Later it got even worse. In his house, I mean. He threatened to kill me. Because the money had been lost. Suddenly I meant nothing to him, apparently. I had this romantic idea . . ."

"Very romantic," Ruff said.

"What do you mean?" she asked, stiffening.

"Slaughtering people isn't exactly romantic."

"Damn you!" Her voice rose and she stepped toward him, both fists uplifted. Ruff was glad those fists were empty and not clutching the hafts of a pair of good knives. She softened suddenly and lowered her hands. She smiled, stepped closer, and kissed Justice.

She kissed him hard, almost angrily. Then she pulled away and said, "We can still be friends."

"Sure."

"Don't you like me?"

"I don't much like killers of either sex."

"Damn you," she shrieked.

Ruff Justice told her, "I'd keep it quiet if I were you."

"Cavanaugh!" Her eyes widened as she looked over Ruff's shoulder into the badlands.

"No. Not yet." Ruff turned and lifted her finger, pointing it for her toward the sinuous band of riding men. "It's Stone Eyes."

"Indians!" She pulled away, turning pale. For a minute Ruff thought her legs were going to give out on her, but she obviously had harder stuff inside her. You don't find the soft ones slitting men's throats. She withdrew carefully from the rim of the ledge. "What do we do?" she asked.

"Wait," was all Justice could tell her. "For now, we wait."

Crouched on the ledge, they watched as the renegade Sioux wound their way into the badlands. They were too close for comfort.

Ruff counted forty of them, but that didn't mean there weren't more somewhere. A good general like Stone Eyes might send his men to a meeting place in different, smaller groups to avoid having the entire band ambushed.

"Are they going the same way we are?" Celia whispered.

Ruff turned to her. "I hope not. It looks like they're going more west once they get over that ridge. Can't tell for sure."

"What will they do?" Celia asked, but Justice was no mind reader and he wouldn't answer that one. He knew what they would do if they found the other whites. They would do what Stone Eyes had sworn to do: kill them all.

"After dark we'll try to move out again," Justice told Celia. It wouldn't be easy traveling, but the moon should be up again to help matters a little. If it didn't cloud up.

"I'm scared, Justice," the lady said as they withdrew a little and sat against the gray stone ledge, watching the distances. "Very scared." Her hand found its way to Ruff's arm and he pulled it away. Lady Celia's face went cold and stiff.

"You forget, lady, I've seen your work."

"You think I'd hurt you?" she asked.

"Only if you got the chance." Justice still had that twenty-five thousand and he didn't figure Celia was above murdering him for that. He didn't think their situation would daunt her in the least. Why not kill Ruff and then hide the money, return to Cavanaugh with some story? If a lady had enough brass, it might work. And this lady had brass.

Still she was beautiful, very beautiful, and as she fell asleep or pretended to, Ruff let his eyes roam her lush body, her golden hair, her peaceful face with its long-lashed eyelids closed, lips slightly curved.

"It's a shame, lady," Ruff said to himself. "A shame that something had to go wrong inside that head of yours."

Ruff pulled away from her then and crossed the ledge alone to watch and wait.

There was no sign of Wadie Cairot and his party. That could mean a lot, not all of it good. Maybe Wadie had taken a different route, maybe he was lying low.

Maybe he had already met up with Stone Eyes.

Ruff checked his weapons out and then settled in. It was going to be a long day with an even longer night to follow.

The moon rose after midnight and Justice got to his feet with a sigh, walking to where Celia rested. She was awake, the light of the golden moon reflected in her eyes.

"Time?" was all she asked, and when Ruff Justice nodded, she got to her feet quickly, silently.

The horse looked up warily as Justice pulled the picket pin, swung the saddle onto its back, and gave the dun its bit.

They started down the long trail, Celia in front of Ruff. The horse picked its own way, making decent time, seeing the trail much better than Ruff could.

There was only one way up and over the ridge unless Justice wanted to turn back toward Cavanaugh's camp, and even Stone Eyes seemed more appealing than that.

As they crested the ridge, the moon seemed to leap into their eyes. The sawtoothed mountains were black and stark above them. Ruff halted the dun briefly and they swung down. Celia crossed her arms beneath her breasts and stared out at the empty land, thinking her own thoughts.

Thoughts of murder? Of wealth?

"You could just let me go," she said, and she turned so that the moon shone on her face. She was a night fairy, a dream woman. Murderess.

"Could I?"

"Sure. Why not?" She smiled and came closer.

"What would you do, Celia? Where would you go?"

"I'd . . ." She seemed to realize only then that there was nowhere left for her to go. Not to England certainly. Not back to Cavanaugh. Nowhere, without the money Justice had in his shirt. That thought seemed to come to them both simultaneously.

"Yeah," Justice said. That was why he still wasn't going to turn his back on this woman.

They rode on. Storm clouds drifted in. The land was shaded briefly and then the panorama of the badlands opened up again as the moon fought back the shadows.

The Sioux were there suddenly.

The Indians expected no such confrontation or they would certainly have seen Ruff first, fired first, but they were tired—it had been a long war trail. There were no soldiers near and no reason to be wary. And they were young, very young.

Ruff crested a low knoll and found their fire, a

small red ember against the dark earth. He saw the two Sioux, both bare-chested, blankets across their shoulders, rise in shock and reach for their weapons.

There was no way to turn the horse and run. Justice slapped his stirrups against the dun's flanks and rode on through the fire, his pistol sending out daggers of flame and death.

One man was hit. The bullet slammed him backward. He performed an awkward half-somersault and then lay still.

The other was luckier or quicker. He flung himself into the brush as Justice's dun leapt the fire and raced on up the canyon. Justice had switched his sights after the first warrior and wasn't able to get off a clean shot.

He fired twice at the rolling blanketed figure that disappeared into the brush. Then the horse's hooves scattered sparks as night went dark and the Sioux was gone.

Ruff turned the dun and stopped, swinging down.

"We've got to keep going," Celia said desperately.

"No. We've got to finish with the Sioux."

If they didn't, then they would be followed, and if they were followed, they would bring death to others, to people like Laura York.

"What can you do?" Celia asked. Fear edged her voice.

"Wait for him," Justice answered grimly. "He'll be coming."

"I want to . . ."

Ruff heard something. He ignored Celia's plaintive complaints, struck the dun on the rump, and let it trot off into the night carrying a reluctant Celia Landis. No matter—let her go, she wasn't likely to wander far, in this country with the Sioux prowling nearby.

Ruff wanted her to go far enough to draw the warrior behind them after her. He drifted into the head-high sage and stood shivering in the night, pistol in hand. When the Sioux came, he came fast. Ruff could hear the labored breathing of the spotted pony he rode, of the warrior himself.

He crouched, waiting.

The Sioux burst out of the night like a demon rising from the broken hills.

Justice leapt from the brush, timing his movement so that he collided with the Sioux's body. The Indian slammed to the ground. His pony danced away, kicking up its heels as the Sioux, rolling, came to his feet. He had lost his gun but he held a knife. Justice leapt back to avoid the lunging Indian blade, but the Sioux missed and it was the only chance he was going to get. Justice tripped the Sioux, and as he went down, Ruff was on top of him. The Indian struggled for possession of Justice's handgun and it discharged into his face, showing a weird, briefly orange glow that disappeared as the muzzle flash was smothered by the night.

Then there was only the warm, still body beneath Justice, and the ringing in his ears.

And out there somewhere fifty or a hundred more Sioux, all of whom had likely heard those shots. It wasn't going to get any easier.

Ruff rose and jogged after the dun horse. He caught up after a quarter of a mile. The dun was standing, head down, its front leg lifted.

"What the hell happened?" Ruff asked Lady Celia.

"He's lame, I think."

Ruff felt its foreleg. A bowed tendon, he

thought—he couldn't tell much in the night. Except that the horse wasn't going to carry them any farther. Ruff stripped the bedroll, shouldered it, and said in disgust, "Let's go. We walk now."

"How far?" Lady Celia asked in a whining voice.

"As far as it takes. Have you got any other ideas?"

She had raised her eyes to the dark hills, a sprawling tangle of land which had somehow seemed passable on horseback but now loomed impossibly. She shook her head in mute surrender, but when Ruff started walking, she followed after him, tucking her skirt up into her waistband.

The moon was cold and bright, too bright. They wove through the scattered sumac and nopal cactus, moving uphill, where Justice figured their chances were better. When it came to a fight, he always chose the high ground.

And Ruff was expecting a fight. Maybe not tonight or in the morning, but the Sioux weren't going to let them out of those hills.

"I can't breathe," Celia said, tripping over a rock. "Justice, can't we stop? Dammit, do you want to end up carrying me?"

"Up there." Justice pointed toward a huge square boulder higher up the mountain. He didn't slow down his pace. Celia Landis had asked for every bit of this.

His own heart was beating heavily, his breath coming in deep gasps when they finally did stop atop the big boulder. He sucked the cool air in, watching the moon-shadowed canyons below them.

"The others—did they get out?" Celia asked.

"No idea. I hope so. We could use a few more guns."

"Against Cavanaugh?"

"Him too," Ruff said.

She was quiet for a minute and Ruff listened to

her breathing. It was quick and shallow and then it turned into a desperate sobbing. He looked at the lady and saw silver tears brim up in her eyes and spill over to run hotly down her cheeks. The moon made it all very tragic and beautiful. That was what Lady Celia was—tragic and beautiful, Ruff decided. But it didn't do to dwell on it.

Half an hour later they rose and tramped on. Ruff's leg muscles had chilled as they sat resting, and now they were sore. Lady Celia had given up complaining, talking. She only trudged on behind the tall man in buckskins—and that was fine with Justice.

He was more worried about Laura York. Laura was a lady worth worrying about. She wasn't any better equipped to take care of herself out there than Celia was. The two men Justice had sent her off with were armed and desperate, but they weren't frontiersmen either.

As they crested the next hill, Justice became more worried, deeply worried. There was fire against the sky. A Sioux encampment lay in the dark rift between two parallel jagged ranges of hills.

There was too much fire. And it lay right in the path they would have to take back to the canyon where Sir Henry had hunted his cougar.

"We have to go around," Celia whispered.

"There's no other way."

"Then back!"

That wasn't much of an idea either. Justice shook his head again. They had only one course of action, and it wasn't something a sane man would relish.

They would have to go *through* the Sioux camp.

17

Celia's face was a mask of astonishment. She wanted to believe she had heard wrong, but Justice's expression was serious. He was going through the Indian camp.

"It's suicide."

"So's going back."

"Maybe we could climb that mountain," she said hopefully.

"In the dark? If we wait till the sun's up, they'll find us, don't you see? We haven't got any choice at all about this."

Celia didn't answer. She was numb with anxiety. Didn't Justice have any nerves? What sort of madman was he? Crazier than Jack Cavanaugh, crazier than Henry, who went around the world looking for new species to kill . . . crazier than she was. She was crazy to have left her home to come here, cold and damp and sterile as it was. Crazy to have traveled here under the illusion that she was saving the American West from the dictatorial rule of a callous government.

Or had that been the real reason? There was something else in her blood, something to do with the thrill of adventure. She needed to be seen as a woman to be reckoned with, to feel the fire in her veins that came with . . . with violence.

The feeling had reached its climax in that little bank in Minnesota when she had shot that clerk to death, four times, even as Wes Savitch grabbed at her, telling her that it was time to go. It had taken her breath away, lifted her to another plane of existence. The savagery found a ferocious chord deep within her and answered it . . .

But *this*—this was something different.

"Let's go. Whatever happens, don't speak," Ruff Justice said. He had yanked the blanket from the bedroll. He stood there, bare-chested now, his long dark hair to his shoulders, blanket around him. He nearly *looked* Sioux. Except for the long mustache. Maybe there was a kinship among these warriors, inexplicable, deeper than blood.

"When we get a little nearer, you're going to have to shuck that skirt. You got anything underneath?"

"Not a damn thing," Celia said, and Justice was pleased to see the spark in her eyes, to hear it in her voice. He didn't want her scared now; he wanted her at her brassiest, her toughest, and she was a tough woman.

"I didn't think you would," Justice said with a smile. "Let's go on down."

They worked their way toward the camp, which was set up among the scattered oaks. Ruff saw the tepees and smoke racks, and nodded with satisfaction. There were women in this camp, and that was important.

As they drew nearer, Celia began to feel the village, to be aware of its scent, of the heat of bodies and fires, of the menace hanging heavily in the air. She sagged a little.

"Straighten up," Ruff said in an undertone,

speaking sharply. "You're tough, aren't you? You're the tough one."

They paused in the oaks, waiting while Celia slipped out of her giveaway skirt.

She hadn't been lying. There was nothing underneath but woman, and if it had been another time, another place ... Justice let his eyes rest on her white thighs, on the dark patch at their junction, and Celia saw him. She smiled faintly, able even now to relish the one true power women have over men.

Justice said, "Rub dirt on your feet and legs. You're too white by far."

Taking his own advice, Ruff smeared dirt on his chest and arms. His face, tanned and nearly as dark as an Indian's needed no special attention. He shifted his weapons, putting his deadly skinning knife in his waistband in front, slipping his Colt in the back of his pants—he wouldn't be needing the pistol. If it came to shooting, then the game would be up. There wasn't a chance in Hades that they would get out of there once the gunfire started.

Ruff looked at Celia, shaking his head at the sight of her yellow hair. There wasn't a lot to be done about that just now.

"Come on," he said, looking toward the Sioux camp, quiet now, needing only a spark to set it off.

"Right through?"

"Right through," Justice said, and sighing a little, he lifted the blanket and wrapped it around his own shoulders, around Celia's shoulders and over her head.

They moved forward as the Sioux camp slept.

Each step was a nightmare. There would be guards out, men watching the camp. Ruff forced himself to make each movement slow and casual. He was a warrior with his woman. Their blanket sheltered them, hiding them from prying eyes. The moon was high. It was a good night for a man to walk out with his woman.

A Sioux appeared from behind a tepee. He turned his head toward Ruff and leaned forward slightly as if trying to identify the man and woman. Then he gave up, turned, and walked away.

The moon bled silver on the earth between the Sioux tepees. An owl hooted from the oaks. Ruff could smell the buffalo meat, smoked and seasoned with sage, the fresh hides, the indefinable scent of a people in turmoil.

Just another few yards—the camp dwindled and merged with the shadow of the canyon beyond. Just a little farther, a few paces.

The Sioux warrior appeared unexpectedly.

He was a friendly man, apparently. He came toward them, speaking a greeting.

Ruff Justice cursed silently, feeling his body tense. He knew a little of the Sioux tongue, but no Indian would ever mistake his voice for one of their own. He let his hand drop to the skinning knife.

"It is a night for walking," the Sioux said again.

"A good night," Ruff Justice answered. His head was down, but the Sioux saw something. Maybe Ruff's mustache, maybe a strand of yellow hair from beneath the blanket, maybe a movement, a wrong gesture . . . The Sioux opened his mouth to cry out and Justice flung the blanket aside, leaping at the warrior's throat.

The Sioux leapt back and Justice's knife slashed at his throat. Together the two men went down, the warrior blocking the second thrust from Justice's blade.

They rolled over in the dirt, Justice tasting bile in his throat, knowing that if the Sioux made a single sound, it was ended, all of it.

The skinning knife tore away three of the Sioux's fingers as Ruff moved upward toward his belly. There was the blood from the severed fingers and then the heavier rush of blood as the blade ripped open abdominal muscle and copper flesh, spilling the Sioux's life out onto the ground.

The brave's mouth opened wide in anguish and Justice covered his lips with his hand, holding it there while the body writhed under him. The skinning knife finished its work, severing the great arteries of the heart.

The man twisted and bucked and finally lay still. Justice rose to stand over his victim, a victim circumstance had hurled into his path—a man he had nothing against, who had been born to die this night beneath the knife of a stranger.

"Let's go. Quickly," Justice said, rising to wipe back his hair.

It couldn't be too quick.

Justice didn't bother trying to conceal the body. Time was too precious. With luck the Sioux wouldn't find the man until morning.

With luck.

They climbed the long canyon behind the Sioux camp, fear and exhaustion combining to make the night a horror as they clambered over rocks, slid down depressions, fought their way through clawing heavy brush, and stubbed their feet on rocks and cactus.

Celia seemed to have gone beyond weariness to some dreamlike state in which she only walked. Nothing else. She wore the blanket wrapped around her hips now. Her yellow hair was a tangle.

Justice said nothing, giving her no guidance. He still had his pistol and the skinning knife, slick with blood. It wasn't enough. A pistol, a knife, and his two feet against Stone Eye's clan, Cavanaugh, and the wilderness.

It wasn't too encouraging.

The sun came from out of nowhere, seeming to leap from the darkness of night to smear the skies with crimson and gold, crowding the valleys with deep purple.

Now they would be seen; now the Sioux were sure to come.

Cougar Canyon seemed impossibly distant. The brush raked against their faces as they clambered up the long slope. The sun was a torment, wringing moisture from their weary flesh. Ruff seldom lifted his eyes to the ridge above them, or the line of blue sky above the hills. He simply climbed.

And from time to time he looked back at the men following them.

They had appeared an hour or so after sunrise, and Celia had noticed them and turned to ask Ruff. She hadn't had to voice her question, nor had Ruff needed to answer.

"Sioux," Ruff said.

The Sioux were definitely on their trail. Strong warriors, they were used to running beneath the hot sun, to fighting under hard conditions. They would run Celia and Justice down easily, given the time.

Celia slipped and fell, banging a knee. She cried out. Justice didn't help her up or urge her on. She knew. Determination and fear lifted her to her feet to walk on, dirty, bloody, the blanket around her hips.

It was hard not to admire her. Ruff wondered what sort of a woman she had been before, when she was a dancer, before this terrible hate had set in.

"The ridge!" Celia cried out in horror, and Ruff

looked up to the hilltop overhead. It was dark, serrated, and seemingly unreachable.

There were two Sioux there, watching, and as Celia pointed her finger, Ruff saw them put their rifles to their shoulders. He threw himself to one side, knocking Celia into the brush as the rifle bullet clipped branches around them and the rolling echo moved down the slope.

A second shot followed but that was the last round to come from that rifle. On one knee, Justice two-handed the big Blue Colt. The revolver kicked, and one of the Sioux tumbled from the ledge, his rifle clattering down the stony bluff.

The second Sioux seemed to disappear as if by magic. But he had to be there still, watching, waiting. Justice looked at Celia's streaked, anxious face and then back down the slope where the pursuing Indians advanced at a steady trot.

"We can't get out. We're going to die," Celia said.

"Giving up?" Ruff asked sharply.

"Why don't you just shoot me now?" she asked. "I don't want them to have me. I've heard the stories."

"Shut up." Ruff was looking toward the bluff. It was sheer and barren. There didn't seem to be a way up that couldn't be covered by a man with a rifle. But if they delayed, there would be guns below as well. Climbing that bluff, a man would become a target in a shooting gallery.

"Well!" Celia shrieked.

"Well . . . we're going up," the tall man told her. His blue eyes were still and nearly peaceful.

"How?"

"We do it, that's all, dammit! You might be satisfied to have me shoot you and leave your hair here for them, but I'm damned if they're going to take Ruff Justice without a fight."

"Tough man, huh?" she asked with scorn.

"Damn right."

Ruff told her what he thought they could accomplish. "There's a narrow chute over there, see it? Behind the screen of brush is where it begins."

Celia looked and nodded. Yes, that could be climbed. She looked anxiously behind them. Ruff took her chin and turned her face.

"Don't look back there. They don't matter, just what's ahead matters, Celia. Do you understand me?" She nodded meekly and he told her, "You're going first. It has to be that way. If the man on the ridge shows, I'll pick him off—or he'll think so."

"What do you mean?" she interrupted.

"Just listen! He knows there are two of us here, a man and a woman. I'm armed. If he rears up, he figures he'll get shot. He's seen I can do some damage with Colonel Colt's invention."

"You want me to risk everything on that. On his being afraid to shoot at me because you might kill him."

Ruffin told her patiently, "He doesn't *want* to kill you, woman. Not just yet."

Her voice was very small. "Oh."

"Yeah, oh. What we're going to do is cross him up." Justice wiped the sweat from his eyes and glanced downslope as a war whoop, still distant, sounded. "Here," he said, and he gave her the Colt.

"What?"

"You make for the chute. I'll watch you go, and when you've counted twenty, I'll start. The Sioux will want me and he'll figure he has me. You keep those sights pointed upward. If he shows, shoot him."

"I can shoot a little . . . but with a handgun!"

Ruff nodded. He was every bit as dubious as Celia Landis, but he had no other ideas.

"Try it. If it doesn't work, we'll both have to learn

171

to fly." Then he winked and Celia almost smiled. She concealed the pistol in her blanket and at Ruff's signal started toward the bluff. Her heart in her throat she raised her eyes to the ridge above them, where death waited in feathers and paint.

The brush appeared like a dark wall and Celia was in it, panting, eyes alert.

She began to count.

At the number eighteen Justice started his run toward her, zigzagging across the ground Celia had just covered. She held the gun overhead, staring up at the dark ridge, the hammer on the big Colt drawn firmly back. Rock dust trickled down along with a single pebble, and when the Sioux appeared, Celia was ready. The bead sight settled on his chest and she squeezed off.

With a scream of pain and terror the Sioux cartwheeled into space. He seemed to fall forever, eyes wide, body smeared with blood before landing sickeningly on the rocks where he lay still and broken.

Justice reached the brush and stood looking at the girl with the big smoking pistol, at the dead Sioux. "Up and over now," Justice said. "If we get over the ridge first, we've a chance."

"Really?" Her green eyes shifted to Ruff, yellow hair drifting across her too-pretty face.

"I think so."

"To get all the way free?"

"That's what we're hoping for. They'll come slowly up this ridge for the same reason we did—they won't be sure that we're not up there ready and willing to snipe at them. Now give me that Colt and let's get going."

"Suppose," Celia said, "we do it my way? Why don't you just give me that money bag, Mister Justice? Or should I take if off your body?"

She drew back the hammer and Justice was suddenly looking down the dark bore of the .44 pistol. She meant to use it. He could see that in her eyes.

"It's no good, Celia."

"Why not?"

"It was all talk. Trying to cheer you up. We can't get out of these hills. You can't, alone. If I give you the money, it won't help you a bit. What are you going to do? Buy your way out?"

"We'll see. Give me that money."

"Or what?"

"You know what. Give me the money sack!"

Her eyes were oddly lighted and Justice knew he wasn't going to talk her into anything sensible. He shook his head and withdrew the sack from inside his shirt."

"Here," he said. "I guess it doesn't matter as long as Cavanaugh doesn't get it. But I guess you never intended for him to have it anyway, did you?"

"It doesn't matter what I intended. Throw the sack down, Justice. Do you think I'm going to try to take it out of your hand?"

Another war whoop, this time an excited yipping, sounded downslope. "They're getting closer, Celia."

"I'll have time."

"You don't even know where you are. How are you going to walk out of here?"

"I've fought tougher odds, Justice. Dragging myself up out of the slums, using men, letting them use me until I found Henry Landis. I thought I was in paradise—at first. But he ignored me. He went away hunting. You know what that means to a woman? To be ignored is the worst thing you can do to us."

Ruff started to move toward her, his hand snaking out, but she jerked away from him.

"Now, you bastard, you're going to die," she said.

"Why?" Ruff's voice was even. "Why kill me, Celia?"

"You know too much about me. Besides, you ignored me too, didn't you? Rejected me and went after that little redheaded slut of a newspaperwoman."

"That's right. At least she *was* a woman," Ruff said very quietly.

The voice from the ridge above them disagreed. Laura York was there and she snapped, "What do you mean *was* a woman! Ruff Justice, I still am one. You, you murdering thing, put that gun down or I'll do what I'm itching to do, kill you."

"Listen—" Celia began.

"You listen, dammit. You've killed my father and you're threatening to kill a man I happen to care a little about. I think you got that Sioux with a lucky shot. I happen to know how to use one of these things fairly well. The best thing you can do is to take your chance with a male jury—assuming we ever do get out of here. Don't think about," Laura commanded, "drop it now—or die!"

18

Ruff Justice saw it in her eyes before Laura could. Celia was willing to die for that money. There was another element involved, one Justice couldn't quite label. This lady wanted to kill; there was an excitement in her eyes, nearly a lust for violence.

She swung around wildly and fired three times, spraying lead across the bluff. She proved that killing that Indian had been a lucky thing by missing all three times. Laura York was cooler.

Her rifle went to her shoulder and spoke once, authoritatively. Crimson spread across Celia's blouse as she was thrown backward, the pistol dropping free. She lay still, instantly dead. The blanket had come unwrapped from her hips, and Justice, moving to her, covered the blonde with it.

This time it wasn't cougar gore that soaked the lady's clothing, and this time there wasn't a thing Justice could do about it.

Laura barked, "Dammit, Justice, let's get going," but her voice was shaky.

Justice picked up his pistol and collected the Sioux's Winchester. Then he climbed the slope to where Laura York stood, windswept, stunned.

"I did it," she said in awe.

"You had to."

"Damn all, Justice," the redhead said. "I think if you don't take me in your arms right now, I'm going to fall down and faint—and that won't do either of us any good."

Ruff held her to him, feeling her shudder with shock and fear in her. The wind was gusting and cold. Laura needed only a minute to regain herself. Abruptly she stepped back.

"Justice, you didn't ever . . ." She was looking at the crumpled woman below.

"No. Never."

"Why not?" The blue eyes were questioning as Laura looked up at Ruff's face.

"I don't know. Maybe I could sense it in her. I don't know." He looked downhill again, seeing the line of painted Sioux warriors. "We'd better get out of here. Where did you come from, anyway?"

"Sorry that I'm here?" she teased.

"As sorry as I am to be breathing, yeah."

"I came back to look for you. It's that simple."

"Alone?"

She shrugged. "The Englishmen didn't seem too eager to double back."

"They had some sense." Justice looked down their backtrail and said, "Let's get out of here."

"I've got horses."

"You do, do you?" He smiled and kissed her forehead. "You're a woman, aren't you? All woman."

"All woman. Let's go. They're about a mile back. I spotted you from up above, saw the Sioux, and knew I wasn't going to ride up on them. It took me almost two hours to wriggle up there."

"You could have shot them," Justice complained.

The lady laughed. "Hell, Ruffin, who do you think got that first brave?"

They slid, ran, and stumbled down the long hill to where the horses were tied. The Sioux were still back there, still gaining, but once they were on horseback, the Indians would be left behind.

That left only a few problems. Like a hundred miles of wilderness and Jack Cavanaugh.

They found Sir Henry and Sir Oswald at Cougar Canyon an hour before dusk. Sir Henry was still shaken, pale, and thin, his eyes too bright. Sir Oswald was worse off. The fat man was dead.

"His heart, I think," Sir Henry said. "Climbing these hills, riding all night, the wounds . . ."

"You could have buried him."

"What?" Sir Henry glanced at his brother. "Oh, yes, I suppose so. It didn't occur to me. Isn't that . . . Where's Celia?"

"Dead."

"I think I knew that she was." The lord got to his feet and stood, rifle in hand, looking across the badlands where the shadows were gathering. "It's best. What happened?"

Laura York said, "I shot her. She was trying to kill Ruff Justice and me."

"Yes," Sir Henry said hollowly. "It's best. Don't feel bad, Miss York. I would have had to do it myself. Honor demands—"

Laura interrupted hotly. "Honor! You know a lot about honor, don't you, Sir Henry? Taking a young woman, marrying her, but scorning her because she was of a different class. Going around the world, leaving her at the mercy of radicals like Cavanaugh, at the mercy of your friends and relatives . . . I hated the lousy bitch! But even I can see a part of what was wrong with her was you!"

Sir Henry just stood, transfixed, staring into nothingness.

Ruff touched Laura's shoulder and said quietly, "Come on, there's no good in this. Let's get the hell out of here."

"Yes," Laura York said. "Let's get the hell out of here. I want my small town and my own bed again, Ruff Justice." And nobody could blame her for that sentiment.

They started down the long canyon, watchful, expectant. There was too much out there, too many savage, killing things.

The flash of color startled Laura York and caused Ruff to lever a round into the chamber of the Winchester. The color was blue. Then there was yellow with it and they could see that there were soldiers in the hills below.

"Cairot." Ruff counted them; they were all there. Billy Sondberg and Reb and even Fritz. He saw Hawk and, straggling after them, Sir Henry's servants, the camp hands, and the wrangler.

"I'll be damned," Ruff Justice said under his breath. Cairot had made it out, but then he had always been a good soldier. Even if he wanted to see Ruff dead on the ground because of his brother's wife.

They rode on slowly and at the place where the canyon mouth opened onto the plains, where the dark river ran, they met, these two desolate parties.

"Made it," Justice noted.

Wadie Cairot nodded. There was still hatred in his eyes, but maybe a little admiration as well.

"See you did too. Lost a couple."

"The woman. Sir Oswald. What happened to Cavanaugh?"

"You wouldn't have wanted to see it." Wadie Cairot looked shaken, though a veteran of many battles. "Stone Eyes got him. Cavanaugh was on our butts. We scooted up a canyon, prepared to make a stand—what kind of stand I could make with these lollipops, I don't know—and Jack Cavanaugh was behind us."

Cairot shrugged. It was growing darker, cooler. He removed his hat and wiped his forehead with his sleeve.

"Yeah?" Ruff nudged gently.

"We rode like hell, best we could anyway with these lollipops." He inclined his head toward the Englishmen. "All of a sudden the Sioux were there. They came out of a side canyon, and Justice, I've seen Indians, but there was a lot of 'em. And crazy as hell. They let us go by—maybe they wasn't in position yet, or maybe they wanted Cavanaugh for walking their hills, I don't know—but they hit Jack and that was all there was to it."

"Wiped them out?" Ruff asked.

"Well, Cavanaugh had him some fighting men and he had him some people that just fancied themselves. They had guns and thought that made 'em warriors. Stone Eyes," Cairot said with respect for his enemy, "had *him* some fighting men."

"Bad, was it?" Ruff asked. He knew. He had seen some bad ones, the kind they called massacres.

Cairot just lifted his eyes briefly and then shook his head.

"What happened?" Sir Henry was wild with excitement or fear.

Cairot grew an inch or two in Ruff's estimation when he answered. "There was war. You know, killing? Hunting. Some blood was spilled. If you ask me another time, I'll draw you some pictures, my lord."

"Now what?" Laura York asked.

"Now," Ruff answered, "we get the hell out of here while we can. Stone Eyes' people will be celebrating their victory soon. They'll be cutting up the bodies and taking the clothing and weapons of the dead. After that, they'll likely go into Cavanaugh's camp and loot it. They won't be too concerned with us right now. I hope. Wadie?" Ruff asked the NCO, who was still nominally in charge.

"We ride. Fast and far," Cairot said. "Justice," he added when it seemed that no one else could hear them, "this don't mean it's over between us. This don't mean that I don't owe you for laying down with Cole's wife."

"His *widow*, Wadie," Ruff corrected him. "Do you think she's going to shun men the rest of her life?"

"His wife. I won't forget," Cairot said, and Justice swallowed the violent answer that rose in his throat.

"Let's get the hell out of these damned, deadly hills," Ruff Justice said.

They rode through the night. The moon, rising a little later, was a cold silver disk in the blue-black sky. Coyotes in large packs howled at the emptiness of the prairie. They rode on.

The horses hung their heads. Men slept in the saddle. Once Fritz yelled out in pain. They clenched their weapons, knowing that Stone Eyes could be back there, that he might come at any moment.

And they rode on.

Nothing had ever appeared so inviting as the bright strand of the Upper Missouri River and the low, jumbled town of Bismarck, Dakota Territory.

Some people had been able to sleep a little even as they rode, but Justice wasn't one of them. His eyes were raw and red and his body wooden.

"Home," Laura York said.

"Yes," Ruff Justice drawled. "And I'm going to hate to have to turn in this report to the colonel. I lost the whole outfit."

"It wasn't your fault. You told them to turn back."

"It was my fault," Ruff said, and for a moment he thought about the dead, about Sir Oswald; about

Honus Hall, whom he never liked but who hadn't really deserved to die; about the lovely blond thing with the green eyes, the porcelain flesh, the teasing laugh—and the incarnadine blood.

"It was," he said mysteriously to Laura, "all my fault." But then maybe he was thinking of another time, another woman, of the Crow girl he had taken to wed, of children unborn.

He didn't speak the rest of the way to Lincoln, and when he had to kiss Laura good-bye at the gate, there was a distance to the kiss, to their knowing each other—a distance Laura would never really understand.

Still she could look at him with a smile and say, "Ruffin T., you are a man. I'll be there, in Climax, waiting if you ever want a steady redheaded woman for your own. And if you don't"—she touched his chin with her first finger—"well, you come by and see me anyway. And damn you if you won't ever."

"I will," he said with a smile. "One day."

And she half-believed him.

After dark the tall man rose from his bunk, shaved carefully, and patted a little bay rum on his face. Then he saddled a pale horse and rode out toward the Brakes. There was a light on in the cabin when Justice swung down. She was waiting at the door, Carrie Cairot, wanting nothing but a good loving man, wanting to feed him and bed him and keep him warm through the night.

"Well, by God, you came back, Ruff Justice."

"I'm back."

She put an arm around him and took him into the house, and Justice ate at her table, ham and corn bread and beans and hot cross buns. And when he was full of supper and drowsy, she rose and took off her clothes.

"Come on, Justice, take me into the bedroom and let's make some of this nasty world go away."

She was healthy and pink and white, and Justice smiled. He wanted her, wanted her badly.

She took his hand and they went into the bedroom. Carrie turned back the patchwork quilt, lay down, and stretched out her arms. "Blow out that lamp," she said, and Justice did so.

He went to her beneath the blankets and she was a warm and loving thing, needing him too.

The gunshot brought them up sharply.

Justice leapt for his gun belt, but it wasn't necessary. There was a soft tap on the door and Justice went to it, pistol held high. It was Wadie Cairot.

"No more, Wadie," Ruff Justice said angrily.

"No more. A man can't stay a fool forever." Then the sergeant nodded his head toward the still figure on the ground outside the window.

"Is he still alive?"

"Barely."

And Ruff Justice went to crouch down over the body of Wesley Savitch. The gunman looked oddly peaceful. "Tried to gun you," he said hoarsely.

"Why, Wes?"

"You killed Rafer." His words came slowly. "And you had the money. Figured you still had it. No one would've known . . ."

"No one would've known. I turned it in, though, Wes."

The dying gunman's eyes opened with surprise. "So you are that kind of man, after all. A fool!"

"Just a fool," Ruff agreed.

"Lucky for you"—he looked at Cairot—"you've got so many friends."

"Lucky for me," Ruff said quietly, and then he and Wadie Cairot watched as the badman breathed his last.

When it was over, Wadie rose and said, "I guess I'll be getting back to the post now."

"Wadie," Ruff asked, "what were you doing out here? What was it *you* came out here to do?"

Wadie Cairot shook his head, looked at the revolver in his hand, and then turned, walking away to where his horse was tied.

Justice watched him go, but it was cold and there was a warm bed and a needing woman inside the house, and he walked back to her, leaving the dead man to the dark of night.

WESTWARD HO!
The following is the opening section from the next novel in the gun-blazing, action-packed Ruff Justice series from Signet:

RUFF JUSTICE #24: FLAME RIVER

1

"They've killed Colonel MacEnroe!"

Ruff Justice rolled slowly toward the bedroom door, his anger at being interrupted colliding with the unreality of the trooper's message. It wasn't true, couldn't be. The commanding officer of Fort Lincoln dead?

"Who killed him, Corporal? What are you talking about?"

The corporal stopped, panting in the doorway to the little house on the Missouri Brakes. His mind was still burning with the shocking information. He was new to Fort Lincoln, but he had heard of Ruff Justice. He'd heard that Justice was the hardest-fighting, hardest-loving, strangest man in Dakota; that he wrote poetry and had toured Europe with Bill Cody, reading his poems to the crown heads; that he and Bill Hickok had once cleaned up a town on a bet; that Ruffin Tecumseh Justice had killed six men in stand-up duels, three of them fighting

Excerpt from FLAME RIVER

the Cajun way, the opponents' wrists lashed together, the fighting done with bowie knives.

Still the corporal hadn't expected to find the lean, long man in bed with a woman who was voluptuous, beautiful, and apparently unashamed. She reflected Ruff's ruddy postcoital complexion, his concern with the news.

Justice was even taller than the soldier had thought, his dark hair curling past his shoulders, his mustache long and curved, his body pale and hard as he rolled from the bed naked.

"What happened, where?" the scout demanded. He was tugging on his fringed buckskin trousers as the woman—the sister-in-law, they said, of a Lincoln NCO named Cairot—dressed hurriedly in a wrapper and slippers.

"I don't know, sir," the young, freckled soldier said. His eyes drifted to the woman. She didn't seem concerned one way or the other.

"Coffee, Ruff?" she asked.

"Not unless you can whip it up in thirty seconds, Carrie, thanks."

The tall man had his shirt on now, his long dark hair, as beautiful as a woman's, brushed back. He had his gun belt on and his big .56 Spencer rifle in its beaded buckskin sheath in his hands.

"I'm going, Carrie."

"All right. Is it true? Can it be true?" the sensuous, soft-looking woman asked.

"I don't know. I hope to hell it's not." Ruff had never known another commanding officer at Fort Lincoln. The silver-haired MacEnroe, was narrow, aristocratic, and opinionated. He had feuded with Ruff frequently, but he had always been a gentleman, always been a soldier.

Excerpt from FLAME RIVER

What more could you ask of a man?

"Let's go, Corporal," Ruff Justice said, pausing long enough to kiss the woman—tasting her warm, hungry lips—before leaving. "I'll be back," Ruff Justice told her.

"I know you will, tall man. If you know what's good for you." She winked then, and Ruff took her hand, squeezing it once before he went out the door, the uniformed soldier ahead of him.

The corporal had a regulation bay horse without a spot of white on it. Justice's horse was a zebra dun with one blue eye.

The plainsman swung aboard, grim and silent. The sky was gray above the Missouri River, the marshes dark green and alive with the sound of frogs. Distantly Bismark made itself known as steamboat whistles sounded and carpenters drove nails, bringing the plains to life.

"Where'd you get the word, Corporal?" Ruff asked. "Who told you MacEnroe was dead?"

"All I know is what the first shirt told me. Lieutenant Strange is the one who brought the word into Lincoln."

"So Mack Pierce sent you out. Why didn't Strange?"

"Lieutenant Strange is in no shape to talk to anyone, sir. He's been shot up bad. He'll be lucky if he makes it," the enlisted man said.

Justice didn't like this, didn't like it at all. Things were supposed to be fairly quiet out on the plains just now. Stone Eyes, a renegade Sioux, had given them some trouble in the past, but he had drifted north, out of their area of responsibility. That was the reason Justice had been able to take a brief leave.

Excerpt from FLAME RIVER

What could have tempted Col. MacEnroe to go out onto the prairie, then? Warrior chief that he was, MacEnroe had become essentially a desk officer. Ruff hadn't seen the colonel take the field in the last eighteen months, not since the great tribes of Red Cloud and Crazy Horse had moved into Canada. The colonel, as most warriors do in time, had gotten tired of war.

This time he had gone out. This time he had paid the warrior's price.

Ruff rode the zebra dun through the gates of Fort Lincoln, the corporal following in a dust storm. Swinging down when they came to the orderly room, Justice tramped in.

Lincoln's first sergeant was a huge bear of a man, patient and imperturbable. Normally. Just now Mack Pierce was pacing the floor of the office, looking like he was about to come apart.

"Ruffin!" he said with relief.

"What's happening, Mack?"

"Lieutenant Donaldson will tell you." Mack nodded toward the colonel's office. "He's acting commander. Since—"

"Where's Strange?" Ruff demanded. "I want to talk to him."

"Doc Simms has him. Better see Donaldson."

Ruff nodded. He didn't care to talk to the smooth-cheeked young lieutenant. He had nothing personal against Lt. Donaldson—by all accounts he was coming along fine—but he wasn't Col. MacEnroe.

Donaldson was greener than Mack Pierce, even more relieved to see the tall, mustached scout.

"Justice!" He rose, knocking over a tin cup of coffee. Donaldson was blond, blue-eyed, thick in the

Excerpt from FLAME RIVER

chest and shoulders. They said he was a powerful man; just now he looked like a scared kid.

"What's happened?" Ruff asked.

"Colonel MacEnroe is dead. Down on the Flame River."

"Who says?"

"Lieutenant Strange. He saw it."

Ruff answered, "I want to talk to Strange."

Donaldson nodded, crossed the room, and took his hat from the hat tree. Together they walked out of the office and into the bright sunlight.

"All I know is what Strange said," Donaldson said. "And Strange . . . won't be able to tell his story much longer."

"That bad?"

"Doc says so. He was shot in the back. The bullet did some lung damage."

Across the parade ground all activity seemed to have stopped. The cavalrymen on the post stood watching Justice. They were silent, stunned.

"What in hell made MacEnroe go out on patrol?" Justice asked.

"The woman, I think, though the colonel wouldn't admit that to the junior officers."

"A woman?" Ruff glanced sideways at the young lieutenant.

"Yes, a civilian with a younger woman as her sole companion. Mother and daughter I think. The older one knew the colonel. She was a handsome thing, tall, graying a little. I guess . . . well, the colonel knew her from somewhere back. She wanted to go through to Cooper's Bend. The colonel said he guessed he'd take her himself."

They had reached the infirmary. Stepping up onto the plankwalk, they went in to smell the ether

Excerpt from FLAME RIVER

and alcohol in the post surgeon's office. Doc Simms lifted bleary eyes, poured himself a drink unabashedly, and drank it down.

"In there," the surgeon said.

They found what was left of Lt. Strange lying flat on his back. His complexion was gray, his eyes sunken. His chest was swathed in bandages; his hands twitched constantly. He saw Justice and tried to sit up.

"The colonel. Got to get back, Justice!"

"All right." Ruff smiled, or tried to. He lowered the injured lieutenant. "What happened, Strange? Slowly."

It took him a hell of a long time to tell it, and some of it didn't make much sense. The man was in pain and half out of his head.

"Mutiny," was what Lt. Strange panted. "It was a mutiny, Justice."

Ruff and Donaldson exchanged disbelieving glances. In the U.S. army, on this post?

"Mutiny. They got me. Killed me. Got the colonel."

"You saw him die."

"Shot him three times. I saw them shoot him."

"Did you see him die, Strange?"

The man turned feverish eyes toward Ruff Justice. "I saw him go down. I went to him. He told me, 'Get Ruff Justice.' That was all he said. 'Get Ruff Justice, Strange. Tell him he has to get the women back.'"

"Strange!" The man had lapsed into semiconsciousness. Ruff touched his shoulder gently. "What the hell happened down there? Where's everyone else?"

His eyes opened again. "Mutiny. Down on the

Excerpt from FLAME RIVER

Flame River. The colonel wants you, Justice. No troopers. Order—no troopers."

That was the last thing Lt. Strange ever said in this life. Justice closed the officer's eyes and stood still for a moment, staring at the patch of light that fell on the wooden floor.

"What are you going to do?" Donaldson asked.

"Do? Get down to the Flame. Find the women. Those were his orders."

"I'll assemble—"

"You'll do nothing," Ruff Justice interrupted him. "Those were a part of the colonel's orders too."

"I have my duty," Donaldson said stiffly.

"Yes. To follow orders. The same duty I have while I'm accepting army pay. Let's not aruge about it, Donaldson. For some reason, the colonel thought I could do this job for him. I mean to try. The best thing you can do is just stay out of my way. Because if it's true that the colonel is dead, there are going to be some men going down in front of my guns before this is over."

SIGNET Brand Westerns You'll Enjoy

(0451)

- ☐ LUKE SUTTON: OUTLAW by Leo P. Kelley. (115228—$1.95)*
- ☐ LUKE SUTTON: GUNFIGHTER by Leo P. Kelley. (122836—$2.25)*
- ☐ LUKE SUTTON: INDIAN FIGHTER by Leo P. Kelley. (124553—$2.25)*
- ☐ LUKE SUTTON: AVENGER by Leo P. Kelley. (128796—$2.25)*
- ☐ AMBUSCADE by Frank O'Rourke. (094905—$1.75)*
- ☐ BANDOLEER CROSSING by Frank O'Rourke. (111370—$1.75)
- ☐ THE BIG FIFTY by Frank O'Rourke. (111419—$1.75)
- ☐ THE BRAVADOS by Frank O'Rourke. (114663—$1.95)*
- ☐ THE LAST CHANCE by Frank O'Rourke. (115643—$1.95)*
- ☐ LATIGO by Frank O'Rourke. (111362—$1.75)
- ☐ THE PROFESSIONALS by Frank O'Rourke. (113527—$1.95)*
- ☐ SEGUNDO by Frank O'Rourke. (117816—$2.25)*
- ☐ VIOLENCE AT SUNDOWN by Frank O'Rourke. (111346—$1.95)
- ☐ COLD RIVER by William Judson. (137183—$2.75)*
- ☐ THE HALF-BREED by Mick Clumpner. (112814—$1.95)*
- ☐ MASSACRE AT THE GORGE by Mick Clumpner. (117433—$2.25)*
- ☐ BROKEN LANCE by Frank Gruber. (113535—$1.95)*
- ☐ QUANTRELL'S RAIDERS by Frank Gruber. (097351—$1.95)*
- ☐ TOWN TAMER by Frank Gruber. (110838—$1.95)*

*Prices slightly higher in Canada

Buy them at your local bookstore or use coupon on next page for ordering.

Other Signet Westerns for you to enjoy

(0451)

- [ ] **CORUNDA'S GUNS** by Ray Hogan (133382—$2.50)*
- [ ] **AGONY RIDGE** by Ray Hogan (131150—$2.50)*
- [ ] **APACHE MOUNTAIN JUSTICE** by Ray Hogan (137760—$2.75)*
- [ ] **THE VENGEANCE OF FORTUNA WEST** by Ray Hogan (129199—$2.25)*
- [ ] **BUGLES IN THE AFTERNOON** by Ernest Haycox (114671—$2.25)*
- [ ] **TRAIL SMOKE** by Ernest Haycox (112822—$1.95)*
- [ ] **CANYON PASSAGE** by Ernest Haycox (117824—$2.25)*
- [ ] **DEEP WEST** by Ernest Haycox (118839—$2.25)*
- [ ] **VENGEANCE RIDER** by Lewis B. Patten (126211—$2.25)*
- [ ] **THE ANGRY HORSEMEN** by Lewis B. Patten (093097—$1.75)
- [ ] **RIDE A TALL HORSE** by Lewis B. Patten (098161—$1.95)*
- [ ] **TRACK OF THE HUNGER** by Lewis B. Patten (110315—$1.95)*

*Prices slightly higher in Canada

Buy them at your local bookstore or use this convenient coupon for ordering.

NEW AMERICAN LIBRARY,
P.O. Box 999, Bergenfield, New Jersey 07621

Please send me the books I have checked above. I am enclosing $_____
(please add $1.00 to this order to cover postage and handling). Send check or money order—no cash or C.O.D.'s. Prices and numbers are subject to change without notice.

Name _____

Address_____

City_____State_____Zip Code_____

Allow 4-6 weeks for delivery.
This offer is subject to withdrawal without notice.